The Governess Is A Lady

THE DARROW SISTERS
BOOK TWO

FIONA MIERS

This is a work of fiction. Similarities to real people, places, or events are entirely coincidental.

THE GOVERNESS IS A LADY

First edition. June 22, 2024.

Copyright © 2024 Harley Romance Publishing.

Contact: harleyromancepublishing@gmail.com

Website: www.harleyromancepublishing.com

Written by Fiona Miers

Chapter One

In the grand ballroom of the Weston estate, fresh flowers perfumed the air while lively music played. The room was alive with the chatter of the ton. Men donned in their finest, women swirling in exquisite gowns. Lady Olivia Darrow, walking amidst them, was notably distinct. It wasn't a lack of grace or beauty that set her apart, rather it was her distinct air of indifference. As she made her way through the sea of guests, this aura clung to her, marking her presence as uniquely her own.

Olivia, the second oldest of the Darrow sisters, was a vision of loveliness in a gown of soft lavender, a tribute to her father's recent passing. She'd worn rags in her hair overnight to ensure soft curls, and waves framed her face, while her hair was braided into a high chignon accessorised with ribbons and pearls.

Despite the opulence that surrounded her, Olivia's gaze was unfocused. Her mind was miles away from the dance of courtship that played out before her.

Eleanor—her older sister and now Lady Weston since her marriage to Lord Weston— made an elegant hostess, moving through the room with a practiced grace, her laughter mingling with that of her guests. The ball, a spectacle to salute their newfound status as Lord and Lady, was as much a celebration of their union as it was a not so subtle marketplace for eligible bachelors and hopeful young ladies.

But where Eleanor found purpose, Olivia found pretence. The idea of marriage to achieve security or improve social standing chafed against her very soul. There had to be something more, a future beyond the confines of whispered agreements and strategic alliances.

Olivia excused herself from yet another tedious conversation about the merits of a suitable match, and tried to ignore whispers that followed her like persistent shadows.

"Lady Olivia seems uninterested in the proceedings tonight," commented one matron, her voice laced with disapproval.

"Indeed. One does wonder if she intends to follow her sister down the aisle at all," her friend responded, the gleam in her eye betraying an appetite for gossip.

At a familiar surge of frustration, Olivia squeezed her fingertips into her palms. The constant scrutiny, the endless speculation about her future were suffocating, as was the atmosphere in this crush. She longed for a breath of fresh air, for a moment of solace away from prying eyes and wagging tongues.

With a polite smile that didn't quite reach her eyes, Olivia made her way to the terrace and breathed in the reprieve of the cool night air. The stars overhead twinkled with a serene indifference to both the drama and the tedium that unfolded beneath them.

She leaned against the balustrade, and the sounds of the ball seemed to fade into the background, replaced by the quiet rustle of leaves and the distant call of a nightingale. Could Olivia dare to dream of a life where her worth was not measured by the title she might acquire through marriage, but by the deeds she could accomplish with her own hands and heart?

Her shoulders slumped. Such dreams were nothing more than fanciful illusions. Society had little use for a woman who sought to define her own path, especially one as unyielding as she.

But Olivia Darrow was not easily deterred. Staring at the night sky, she made a promise to herself. She resolved to find her own way, to carve out a space where she could be true to herself. Perhaps, in the vast, unpredictable tapestry of life, there would be a place for a woman like her—a woman who dared to imagine a life beyond the ballroom, beyond the confines of marriage.

The soft rustle of silk announced the presence of another. She turned to find Eleanor approaching, concern etched upon her features.

"I was hoping to find you here." Eleanor touched her arm. "I know these events are not to your liking, Olivia. I cannot thank you enough for being here tonight to support me and the family despite your reservations."

Olivia offered a small, wry smile, appreciating her sister's understanding. "Just because you've become Lady Weston doesn't mean you—or I—have to play by society's rigid games." She couldn't quite keep the defiance out of her tone.

Eleanor's expression shifted, her gaze narrowed. "Unfortunately, that's exactly what it means," she countered firmly. "Especially if we want our brother to be welcomed with open arms."

At the mention of their brother, Olivia's composure faltered. She clenched her jaw, a visible sign of the turmoil that the topic stirred within her.

"No." The word slipped out like a blade. "That's impossible. No one will embrace him. He's our father's illegitimate child, the reason Mother won't leave her room. The societal and legal restrictions placed on illegitimate children means Alexander can provide for him materially, but he will still face significant social stigma and be barred from the line of succession for titles and associated landed estates. Society will shun him just as they shun everyone else who doesn't fit rigid rules."

Eleanor sighed as she reached out to play with a lock of Olivia's hair, a gesture of comfort in the face of the challenge before them. "The weight of our family's scandal rests heavily upon our shoulders."

"Our father's scandal, you mean?" Olivia didn't return Eleanor's gaze or touch. "The reality of the situation is inescapable. The stain of scandal will not easily be washed away by titles or wealth. In the eyes of society, our brother's existence is a transgression, but acknowledging the child into the family amounts to an unforgivable sin, one that could overshadow even a sterling reputation and tar our sisters too."

"I know it," Eleanor murmured. "Even so, we must try. It is the right thing to do and is what we all agreed."

They lingered on the edge of the terrace, silent yet enjoying the reprieve from the crush in one another's company.

Eleanor nudged Olivia. "If you could do anything you wanted, Liv, without worry of judgment or obligation, what would it be?"

It was such a soft invitation for Olivia to share a piece of her true self, how could she resist? After a moment's reflection, her eyes lit up with a passion that seldom found its way to the surface. "I would read. I would sit in the grandest library and devour every book within reach, from dawn until dusk."

Eleanor's expression softened, though she drew her brows together. "That sounds lonely."

Olivia shook her head, a gentle smile curving her lips. "On the contrary." She sighed as she envisioned the very scene she described. "In those pages, I meet new people with every turn. I live a thousand lives, visit a thousand worlds. The characters I encounter become friends, rivals, mentors. Through books, I'm never truly alone."

"As much as you love books, wouldn't you grow weary of them?" Eleanor asked. "Surely, life holds more for you than pages and ink."

"I prefer stories to people." Olivia swallowed. She rarely voiced this depth of feeling. It was an admission, not of disdain but of discomfort —a preference for the quiet companionship of stories over the unpredictable tumult of social engagements.

"This much I know." Eleanor crossed her arms. "You have a line of young gentlemen eager to dance with you, and yet you refuse to so much as acknowledge them."

"They are much more interested in the settlement I'm promised from Lord Weston, rather than me. I'm not interested in—"

"Marriage, yes." Eleanor finished for her. "But what about love?"

A possibility Olivia had considered in the abstract but never dared to explore. She didn't want to live her whole life as a spinster, but marriage meant losing her independence, losing herself. She turned to Eleanor. "Can I have one without the other?"

"I'm not sure." Eleanor hummed thoughtfully. "I suppose it depends on what you and your partner want. It's a discussion to be had between you and that person."

"And what if he wants marriage and I don't?" Olivia pressed.

"Well, I suppose you'll cross that bridge when you come to it," Olivia smiled, it was just like Eleanor to be both pragmatic and romantic. "I'm not asking you to marry, nor am I asking you to fall in love. I'm simply asking you to dance."

"Dance?" Olivia lifted her brows in question.

Just dance. Without the pressure of expectations. Without the inane overly polite chat that seemed to accompany most of them. The simple word seemed foreign in the context of their conversation.

Eleanor nodded, her gaze softening. "Yes, just dance. Allow yourself a moment of freedom, of joy, without the weight of obligations or expectations. Who knows? You might find a kindred spirit on the dance floor, someone who sees the world as you do."

The idea was absurd yet strangely appealing. An invitation to step outside her comfort zone if only for the duration of a tune. Eleanor was not asking her to change who she was, merely to open herself to the possibility of connection, however fleeting.

Perhaps, in the grand scheme of things, a dance was a small concession to make. A chance to experience the music and movement that seemed to bring others so much pleasure. In the safety of her sister's request, Olivia found the courage to entertain the notion.

"All right." Olivia nodded. She had taken dancing lessons after all, and quite enjoyed them. "I'll dance."

Eleanor's smile was radiant. Arm in arm, they returned to the ballroom.

Olivia allowed herself to be led onto the dance floor by the first of her suitors, a young man with striking blue eyes and hair the colour of polished mahogany. He moved with such practiced grace, he must have attended dozens of balls and danced with hundreds of young ladies. His smile was charming, his conversation sprinkled with compliments and light banter, yet Olivia found her mind wandering. She smiled politely, nodding at appropriate intervals, but the vibrant colours of the ballroom blurred into a monotonous palette as she danced in his arms. At least the dancing lessons had paid off. She followed the delicate choreography of the Quadrille without thought, her responses automatic.

The second gentleman was taller, with sharp, angular features and dark eyes that sparkled with intelligence. He spoke of travels to distant lands, then turned to books she had read and loved when he realised she had read so broadly. Yet for all his attempts to bridge the gap between them with words and shared interests, there was no spark of connection, no stirring of interest beyond a fleeting curiosity. She kept her smile slight, a perfect mask that hid her disinterest as she moved through the motions.

By the time the third suitor took her hand, Olivia had perfected the art of the courteous dance partner. This one had a roguish charm, with a quick smile on his handsome face and a twinkle in his eye, suggesting a penchant for mischief. His laughter was infectious, and for a moment, she almost caught herself enjoying the English country dance. But she soon realized the enjoyment was superficial, born of novelty rather than genuine interest. He was just another face in the crowd, another polite, well-intentioned gentleman in a line of many, none of whom could ignite the spark of true engagement in her heart. Her smile, though flawless, was as empty as the conversation.

As the final notes of the evening's last dance faded into silence, Olivia was more than ready to exchange the stifling confines of the ballroom for the quiet solitude of her own room. The night had been a parade of faces and names, each dance blending into the next until they were all but indistinguishable. Olivia's growing sense of detachment was just a reaffirmation of her distance from the world her sister navigated with such ease.

It was blessedly quiet in her room, the familiar scent of leather-bound books welcoming. The heroes of her novels and the gentlemen she had danced with that evening were nothing alike. Her literary heroes were gallant and complex, their virtues and flaws rendered in vivid strokes that invited empathy and understanding. They were men of action and passion, capable of deep love and grand gestures. In contrast, the men of her real-world encounters seemed to be cut from a different cloth, any semblance of genuine emotion or depth carefully guarded, if present at all.

No doubt Eleanor's happiness kindled some hope within her. Somewhere, amid the throngs of eligible bachelors, there might be one whose soul resonated with hers. Her maid helped her out of her gown and took down her hair with the barest of murmurs. Already Jane was attuned to Olivia's moods and knew when to talk and when to hold her tongue.

Olivia settled into the comforting embrace of her favourite chair, a book in hand, and conceded that finding love in real life was a far more daunting task than falling for the hero in a well written story.

In books, love was a grand adventure, fraught with peril but always rewarding. In society, it was so bound up in pretence and polite words, genuine connection was as elusive as a unicorn.

With a soft sigh, Olivia turned her attention to the pages before her. Here, in her private sanctuary, she could lose herself in tales of love and valour, a silent observer to the kind of passion and depth that her real-life encounters had yet to offer.

Chapter Two

In the quiet hours of the morning, James Montgomery, the Duke of Wallingford, wandered through the sprawling corridors of his ancestral home, a grand manor that had stood for centuries as a testament to his family's enduring legacy. The early light filtered through the tall, mullioned windows, casting long shadows on the polished floors, and illuminating the dust motes dancing in the air. The manor, with its imposing stone façade and intricate tapestries adorning the walls, spoke of power and prestige, yet to James, it whispered tales of solitude and memories long past.

His steps echoed in empty hallways, a stark reminder of the loneliness that was his constant companion since the death of his beloved Lady Elizabeth six years ago. The laughter and warmth that once filled these rooms seemed like echoes from another life, leaving behind a profound silence. James moved through the familiar spaces, the weight of his title and the expectations that came with it pressing heavily upon his shoulders. He needed a male heir. It was the one thing his ancestors relied on him to deliver. But how could he ever find another woman to replace her? The manor, for all its grandeur, felt more like a mausoleum than a home, a place where joy had once lived but now only memories resided.

The library, with its towering shelves laden with books, was a sanctuary of sorts for James. Here, amid the scent of aged leather and parchment, he found solace in the written word where the real world offered none. His ancestors had thirsted for knowledge, each volume carefully selected and cherished by generation after generation.

Normally, James enjoyed a treatise on agricultural improvements as much as the latest Jane Austen novel. Yet, as he traced his fingers over the spines of the books, a keen edge of isolation pervaded his thoughts. The stories within those pages spoke of love and adventure, of connections forged in the crucible of shared experiences—things that seemed increasingly foreign to him.

As he continued his solitary walk, James found himself in the drawing room, the morning light casting the furniture in a soft, golden hue. This room, designed for gatherings and celebrations, had once been the heart of the manor, alive with the sound of music and conversation. Now, it served as a stark reminder of what was lost. The portraits of his ancestors looked down upon him, their faces etched with the strength and resolve that had defined the Wallingford lineage. In their silent vigil, James sensed an expectation, a demand to carry forward the legacy of his title, even as his personal world crumbled around him.

The gardens, once his wife's pride and joy, lay just beyond the French doors, their beauty untamed and wild in her absence. James hesitated at the threshold, the pain of his loss sharp as ever. The roses she had tended with such care now grew unchecked, their blooms a riot of colour against the manicured lawns. Stepping outside, he was enveloped in the scent of flowers and the fresh, crisp air of the morning. Here, amidst the beauty she had cultivated, James felt closest to her, the memories of their life together both a salve and a torment to his soul.

As he stood in the garden, the sun rising to herald the start of a new day, James grappled with the realization that time moved inexorably forward, even when the heart remained anchored in the past. The challenge before him was clear: to find a way to live again, not just as a duke, but as a man who still had much to offer, both to his daughter and to the world beyond the gates of his grand yet lonely estate.

As James turned back towards the manor, the tranquillity of the morning was punctuated by a distant commotion that stirred a rare smile on his otherwise sombre face. The source of the disturbance was unmistakable: Charlotte, his precocious ten-year-old daughter, was awake. Her energy and inquisitiveness had a way of breathing life into the staid halls of the estate, a reminder of the joy that once pervaded its rooms.

Stepping through the grand entrance, James's smile faltered as he nearly collided with Mrs. Rutherford, Charlotte's governess. Her face was pinched in frustration, a stark contrast to the mirth he felt moments before. "The girl is too bold, Your Grace," she declared without preamble. "She asks incessant questions, challenges everything. I will not tolerate it any longer."

"Isn't that your job?" James retorted, his eyebrows arching in surprise. "To answer her questions? To teach her?"

Mrs. Rutherford's lips thinned. "She's impossible. She cannot be taught." Her tone brooked no argument.

James couldn't suppress a flicker of amusement from showing on his face. "She's ten." Charlotte's age alone should absolve her of any charges of malicious intractability.

"Exactly my point," Mrs. Rutherford snapped. "Think of how she will behave when she gets older. No. I cannot do it, regardless of the salary. You'll have to teach her yourself. I doubt you'll find anyone who can tolerate her.

Mrs. Rutherford swept past him, her departure leaving a palpable void in her wake. James stood in the foyer blinking slowly. He refused to believe that Charlotte could not be taught. Charlotte's vibrant spirit was not something to be quelled but rather nurtured.

At least, that was what Elizabeth would have insisted upon, even if it was rather troublesome.

The governess' departure marked a turning point, a challenge laid bare before him. If Charlotte didn't cease her challenging behaviours, she would have difficulty fitting into society. That much was true.

But he did not wish to temper her spirit.

As James stepped into the dining room, his gaze immediately fell upon Charlotte, deeply engrossed in her drawing at the table. The sight of her, so focused and content in her own world, softened the edges of concern that had creased his brow moments earlier. Her creativity knew no bounds, a constant source of wonder.

At the sound of his approach, Charlotte's head snapped up, her face breaking into a beaming smile. With the unbridled enthusiasm unique to children, she abandoned her artistic endeavour and rushed to greet him, her small arms wrapping around him in a warm, if somewhat impetuous, hug.

Taking a moment to return the embrace, James then steered her back towards the table, his expression growing more serious. "Charlotte, we need to talk about your behaviour with Mrs. Rutherford." He aimed for a tone that was firm yet not unkind.

Charlotte, however, was quick to express her disdain, her youthful impatience shining through as she rolled her eyes dramatically. "Mrs. Rutherford is so boring," she protested, her voice laced with the blunt honesty of childhood. "I barely paid attention to the lessons at all."

Charlotte, it's important to show respect and to pay attention, not just during your lessons, but all the time." James knelt to be at eye level with Charlotte, his expression softening. "These aren't just rules for the classroom, but for life. Being respectful and attentive helps us learn from others and shows them we value what they have to say."

"But why?" She cocked her head to the side. "Mrs Rutherford wouldn't teach me anything I wanted to learn."

James stifled a chuckle at his daughter's candid appraisal, though he knew the matter at hand was no laughing matter. He ruffled her hair in an expression of exasperation and affection. "I have no idea what I'm going to do with you."

The challenge of finding a suitable governess for Charlotte loomed larger than ever. Mrs. Rutherford was the last in a long line of highly recommended governesses who had come and gone.

He had to find someone who could not only teach her how to manage her behaviour but also engage her mind and spirit. Charlotte needed a governess who was patient but capable of nurturing her insatiable curiosity.

He gazed at Charlotte, her eyes alight with intelligence. The journey ahead would be one of discovery for both. He was determined to find someone who could guide Charlotte's education in a manner befitting her spirited nature, and would appreciate and foster the bright, inquisitive mind of his daughter. In that moment, James vowed to himself to do whatever it took to ensure Charlotte's light would not be dimmed but allowed to shine as brightly as it was meant to.

Charlotte's face brightened, her previous frustrations momentarily forgotten. "Papa, can we go riding today?" She laced her voice with hope.

James hesitated, torn between the desire to indulge his daughter and the pressing responsibilities that awaited him. "I must work today, Charlotte," he replied with gentle regret. "In fact, I'm to meet with some school acquaintances for lunch. Mrs. Hartford will watch you."

Another thing he needed to fix. It wasn't appropriate for the daughter of a duke to help the cook in the kitchen. But he had no sisters, and Charlotte's aunts on her mother's side were in the far North of the country, in Carlisle which was three days travel away. Charlotte was starved of suitable female companionship. What was he to do?

Charlotte's disappointment was swift, but it vanished almost as quickly as it appeared, replaced by another burst of enthusiasm. "Ooh! All right. Maybe I can help her make sweet rolls for afternoon tea."

James watched her, a sigh escaping him. Charlotte's adaptability and ever-shifting focus were both a source of joy and a reminder of the challenge he faced. She needed guidance, yes, but also the freedom to explore and express herself in ways that traditional education—and traditional governesses—seemed ill-equipped to handle.

As Charlotte chattered on about the kinds of sweet rolls she hoped to make, James's thoughts drifted to the task ahead of him. Where on earth would he find a suitably qualified lady capable of nurturing Charlotte's vibrant spirit while providing the structure she needed to learn how to join society as Lady Charlotte in both essence and name.

Chapter Three

The next day, as the evening sun cast a warm glow through the windows of the Darrow family dining room, the atmosphere was filled with the familiar sounds of familial chatter and the clinking of silverware. At the head of the table, Lord Weston presided with a quiet dignity that had become more pronounced since his marriage to Eleanor.

Caroline, Olivia's younger sister, was aflutter with curiosity and excitement, her eyes sparkling with the prospect of hearing about the ball. "Olivia, you simply must tell us everything about the ball! Who was there? Did you dance with anyone interesting?" she asked, her questions tumbling out in a breathless rush.

Across from her, Mary, the youngest of the Darrow sisters, was engaged in her own silent rebellion, about what Olivia had no idea. Her mouth was set in a stubborn line as she pushed her vegetables around her plate with disdain that only a child could muster. Her lack of interest in the conversation was matched only by her determination not to eat what was before her.

Amidst this familiar domestic tableau, Olivia found herself recounting the events of the ball with a detachment that surprised even her. She spoke of the attendees and the music, the dances, and the decorations, all the while feeling as though she were describing a scene from one of her books rather than her own life. Her heart wasn't in the recounting. The ball, for all its splendour, had felt hollow to her, a pageant in which she played a part but did not truly belong.

As supper ended, Alexander's voice cut through the conversation. "Olivia, would you please join me in my study? There's something I'd like to discuss with you."

The sudden seriousness of his tone brought a hush over the table, and all eyes turned to Olivia. A flutter of uncertainty filled her chest at the summons.

Olivia's gaze met Eleanor's across the table. Her elder sister gave her a nod and an encouraging smile, a silent message of support that bolstered Olivia's spirits. Whatever Alexander wished to discuss, Olivia felt a measure of comfort knowing that Eleanor believed in her. That she had her sister's backing.

With a deep breath, Olivia nodded in assent to Alexander's request. As her sisters resumed their conversation, Olivia's mind raced with possibilities. Alexander was a man of few words, and his request for a private audience was unusual enough to pique her curiosity and trepidation.

Olivia followed Lord Weston to his study, a room that reflected the man himself—meticulous, ordered, and steeped in a quiet sense of authority. The heavy oak door swung open to reveal a space lined with bookshelves, each filled with volumes that ranged from ancient texts to modern treatises on law and philosophy. The room was dimly lit by a brass desk lamp casting a warm pool of light over the papers and documents that lay neatly arranged on the mahogany desk. In the corner, a globe and a telescope spoke of a curiosity about the world beyond, while a large window offered a view of the estate's sprawling gardens, now shrouded in the twilight.

As she entered, the soft creak of the leather armchair behind the desk announced Alexander seating himself. He looked up, his expression serious but not unkind, gesturing for Olivia to take a seat in one of the chairs facing the desk. The study felt like a sanctuary of sorts, insulated from the rest of the household's hustle and bustle, a place where important conversations could unfold in privacy and without interruption.

Olivia crunched her hands together in her lap, working up to asking what he wanted her for.

But Alexander beat her to it. He leaned forward slightly, his hands clasped together on the desk, gathering his thoughts before he spoke. "I had lunch with an old school friend today, Duke Wallingford. He's found himself in a bit of a predicament. His governess has left them unexpectedly, and he's struggling to find a suitable replacement for his young daughter."

Olivia listened, a crease forming between her brows as she tried to connect the dots between Alexander's luncheon and her sudden summons to his study.

"I'm not sure what his predicament has to do with me," she murmured.

Alexander met her gaze, his expression earnest. "Eleanor worries about you."

"Yes, I know." Olivia still grappled with the relevance of Alexander's narrative to her own situation.

"I take it you didn't meet the love of your life at the ball last evening?" Alexander asked, a slight upturn at the corner of his mouth suggesting a blend of sympathy and jest.

Olivia blinked, taken aback by the sudden shift in the conversation. The constant changing direction gave her a sense of whiplash, a bewildering transition from Eleanor worrying, to a Duke's domestic issues to her personal life in the span of a few heartbeats.

She answered after a brief pause. "No, I didn't."

She leaned forward. "Why are you asking me such odd and unrelated things?" Her brows knit together in confusion. "This conversation feels like a riddle, each piece of a puzzle floating just out of reach."

Alexander gave her a nod. "You've always been astute, Olivia." He regarded her with a level of respect and understanding that had always characterized their interactions. "I know you've never been one to shy away from chasing what you want, and refusing what you don't." He paused for a moment, ensuring his words had taken hold. "I'm aware that you have no desire to make your launch into society despite your age and the ton whispering about it, nor do I believe you care much about the latest bachelors in want of a wife."

"I'm nineteen, not eighty." Olivia exhaled, a soft chuckle escaping her lips despite the seriousness of the conversation. "I curtsied to the Queen as Lady Beatrice insisted. But I'm so uncertain about marriage at all, let alone with any man I've yet met. My independence is important to me. But I still don't understand what your friend's situation has to do with me."

Alexander leaned back in his chair, a gesture that signalled he was about to delve into a more personal narrative. "Let me tell you about my friend, James." His tone shifted to one of sombre reflection. "His beloved Duchess, Elizabeth, died when his daughter was only five years old, leaving him to raise their daughter, Charlotte. Rather than send her to a female relative or leave her on his estate with a nanny, he took himself, his grief, and the baby girl to his country estate, where they have both stayed for much of the past five years." He paused for a moment, allowing the weight of the story to settle in the room. "James, much like yourself, doesn't hold the ton in high regard. Given your shared perspectives, I believe the two of you would get on quite nicely."

Olivia's immediate reaction was one of scepticism, her eyes rolling at the implication. "Is this your attempt at matchmaking me with one of your desperate colleagues?" She laced her voice with incredulity. "Alex, we may be family, but please don't misunderstand me. I have no intention of marriage—"

"I don't want you to marry the Duke of Wallingford." Alexander interrupted her flow, a twinkle in his eye betraying a hint of amusement at her assumption. "I want you to work for him."

Olivia's mouth curved into a circle. Alexander's suggestion was not a proposal of marriage, but rather an offer of employment, a concept so far removed from the trajectory Olivia had envisioned for herself that it took her a moment to fully comprehend its implications. Employment for a lady in her position was unthinkable.

There could be no question of a genuine paid job. Yet the idea of working for the duke's daughter as a governess—or in some capacity that involved her care and education—was a novel proposition, one that challenged Olivia's preconceived notions about her place in the world and what she was meant to do with her life.

A seed of possibility took root in Olivia's mind, growing tendrils of curiosity and contemplation. The implications of Alexander's suggestion were manifold, challenging her to reconsider the contours of her future in ways she hadn't previously entertained. Working as a governess, with the care of a precocious young lady in her hands, was a departure from anything Olivia had envisioned for herself. Yet, the prospect sparked an unexpected intrigue within her, a flicker of excitement at the thought of stepping into a role that demanded more of her intellect and spirit than society's endless balls and superficial engagements ever could.

With the initial shock of the proposition waning, Olivia leaned in, her practical nature coming to the forefront. "Tell me more about young Lady Charlotte and what would be expected of me."

Alexander nodded, visibly pleased by Olivia's interest, and drummed his fingers against the desk, ready to dive into the details. "Charlotte at age ten is a spirited child, full of insatiable curiosity." His eyes lit up as he spoke of the girl. "These traits, while wonderful, have proven to be quite challenging for the previous governesses."

"So, my hunch was right—Lady Charlotte really is a precocious one, just like I was. Teaching my sisters has given me a good primer on what to expect. Caroline and Mary thrive on tossing complex questions my way, delving into literature, science, history—whatever they suspect might stump me. And the rules? We're always in a debate. They demand to know the 'why' behind every rule I set, challenging me with arguments that really test my logic. I can't help but see a bit of my younger self in both my sisters. I too was often chided for being too keen to show off my knowledge and outsmart my tutors."

Alexander drummed his fingers again. "The experience you've had with your sisters is helpful. Charlotte needs guidance and education, of course, but what she needs even more are companionship and understanding. These are all qualities I've seen in you, Olivia. You have an abundance of them."

Catching Olivia's eye to gauge her reaction, Alexander added, "The role would require a great deal of patience and creativity on your part.

Charlotte must be engaged on her terms, her growth fostered in a way that doesn't stifle her spirit but rather encourages it to flourish."

As Olivia listened, she found herself weighing the realities of such a commitment against her own desires for independence and purpose. The role offered a chance to apply her intellect and compassion in a tangible way, to make a meaningful difference in a child's life. Yet, it also posed questions about her own future, her autonomy, and how this choice might shape the narrative of her life in unforeseen ways.

The conversation with Alexander marked a pivotal moment for Olivia, a crossroads between the life expected of her and the life she might dare to choose for herself. The details Alexander provided painted a picture not just of a job, but of an opportunity—a chance to step beyond the confines of expectations and into a role that promised challenge, fulfilment, and the possibility of finding a sense of belonging and purpose she had long craved.

"Yes." She breathed out. "I'll do it."

Chapter Four

Three days had passed since James' luncheon with Lord Weston, where an unconventional solution to his governess dilemma had been proposed. Alexander, ever the dramatist, had suggested something —or rather, someone—that James found both intriguing and slightly absurd. The thought of bringing Lady Olivia Darrow, Weston's sister-in-law and an eligible lady of the ton, into his home as a governess was unconventional, to say the least.

He knew nothing of the lady. But he was desperate to find a suitable companion and mentor for Charlotte, and Alexander had been at his most enthusiastic and charming best. James was swayed, Alexander wouldn't lead him astray. Besides, he was willing to try anything for his daughter's sake, even if it meant trying the unusual.

The manor buzzed with activity in anticipation of Lady Olivia's arrival. James had ordered a thorough cleaning of the guest rooms with the best view of the gardens for the young woman. He hoped the sight of the lush greenery and the meticulously tended flower beds would make her feel welcome and at ease. A shiver travelled the length of his spine. The well-being and education of his daughter were soon to be in the hands of someone different from the governesses they were accustomed to. The thought both excited and unnerved him.

She was a keen reader, so Alexander told him. This inspired James more than anything. Since the time she could read, and Charlotte developed that skill at a young age, she scorned the nursery and spent much of her time in the library exploring worlds beyond her grasp through books. She'd been reading since she was four and instead of passing the task to a servant, James took extra care to organize the shelves, making sure that literature suitable for both her age and voracious intellect was within easy reach.

An image of Lady Olivia and Charlotte spending hours here, engrossed in stories and lessons that would ignite the young girl's imagination even further brought a smile to his face as he placed a few more volumes on the lower shelves.

The groundskeepers ran throughout the gardens making sure they were immaculate, not just for Olivia's benefit but to provide a vibrant and inviting space for Charlotte to learn and play. The estate, vast and sometimes overwhelming in its beauty, was a testament to the generations of care and attention it had received. James hoped that it would serve as an inspiring backdrop for Charlotte's lessons, offering both teacher and pupil a canvas as boundless as their potential.

James found himself inspecting every corner of the manor, ensuring that everything was in order. The staff, curious about the new companion for Charlotte and as hopeful as James about the changes her arrival might bring, moved with a renewed sense of purpose. He couldn't help but feel a mixture of anticipation and anxiety. Alexander's solution to his problem was unconventional, yes, but James was ready to welcome the change. For Charlotte's sake, he was willing to embrace this new chapter, hopeful that Lady Olivia's presence in their lives would bring the light and laughter that had been missing from the manor for far too long.

Despite his preparations and the hopeful anticipation that filled the manor, he couldn't shake a lingering sense of doubt. The idea of entrusting Charlotte's education and well-being to Lady Olivia, gnawed at him. He questioned whether someone accustomed to the comforts and conventions of London society life could adapt to the realities of raising a spirited child in the countryside. Could Olivia truly connect with Charlotte, offering the guidance and understanding she required?

James worried that Alexander's dramatic flair for problem-solving might have led them down a path fraught with complications. Yet, the possibility of a positive change for Charlotte, the chance to see her thrive under Lady Olivia's care, compelled him to set aside his reservations, clinging to the hope that this unconventional choice was the right one.

On the eve of Lady Olivia's arrival, the manor was cloaked in quiet anticipation, its usual rhythms disrupted by the final flurry of preparations. Duke Wallingford was engrossed in papers from his estate manager. He looked up in surprise when his daughter swung the door open and stepped inside.

"Why is everyone at sixes and sevens just because a new governess is coming?" Charlotte glared at him with arms folded and suspicion in her gaze.

Setting aside his work, he gestured for her to come in. "It's because this new addition isn't actually a governess, she is rather different to the others." He tried to mask his own apprehension about the change.

"I don't want a new governess." She jutted out her chin, her voice tinged with defiance. "Why can't you teach me?"

Her question, innocent yet fraught with longing, struck a chord in James's heart. He sighed, the weight of his responsibilities pressing down on him. "I wish I could, Charlotte, but I can't ignore the demands of the estate. Nor can I guide you as a young lady should be led." He wanted nothing more than to be the one to guide and teach her, to be present in all the small moments of discovery and learning, but the demands of his title and the estate left him little time for anything else, and Charlotte needed to learn the lessons that would prepare her for life as a duke's daughter.

"You always have work to do," Charlotte snapped, her frustration breaking through. "And none of them teaches me a thing."

James felt the sting of her words, a poignant reminder of the delicate balance between duty and fatherhood he struggled to maintain. She had no idea how perilous their situation had been after his father ignored the estate and left it earning less than it cost to maintain.

"I'm sorry I don't get to spend more time with you. But I do enjoy my work, and it allows me to provide for your future, which is very important to me."

Charlotte tilted her head slightly. "My future?"

James took a moment, searching for the right words to explain the complexities of inheritance laws and his responsibility to his young daughter. "I work today so the estate is healthy, and to expand investments to ensure you're taken care of." He pulled her into his lap. A cousin would inherit if James had no son. He might look after Charlotte, but he couldn't count on it, especially if the estate was bleeding money. "You can't inherit the estate, my love, so I must ensure your security for when I'm no longer here."

Charlotte's expression changed, a flicker of understanding passing through her eyes. "Like Mama?"

James' heart squeezed at the mention of her mother, the pain of loss still sharp as ever.

"Yes." He had to swallow several times to get his voice under control. "Things happen sometimes, accidents and illnesses from which we can't save ourselves." In that moment, the distance between them seemed to close, shared sorrow and love bridging the gap as they faced the uncertain future together.

Charlotte hugged him back, then pulled away and settled a searching gaze on his face. "So, how is this new governess different? What makes you think she and I will get on?"

James shook his head slightly at her quick adaptability, a rueful smile touching his lips. "She is the sister-in-law to a good friend, Lord Weston. He tells me that she is well taught herself and loves learning. She is not a trained governess but a lady companion who can teach you both the ways of society and lessons that interest you. He tells me she is quite brilliant and eager to work with you." He paused, choosing his words carefully. "This is why it's imperative that you're on your best behaviour. She is set to come tomorrow, and you must be well-presented."

Charlotte pondered this for a moment, her brows furrowing in thought. "I think I should just be myself," she declared with a hint of defiance. "Then she'll know one way or another if she can even handle me."

James's expression turned serious, and he took her hand in his. "Given your history with governesses, that's a terrible idea. Please, Charlotte. It's important that we give Lady Olivia a chance. I need you to do this for me."

Charlotte gave her father a long, weighted look.

Did she understand the weight of his plea? It was more than a simple call for good behaviour, it was a plea for understanding and cooperation, a hope that she could see beyond her immediate desires and recognize the importance of this opportunity for them both.

That night, as the manor settled into deep silence, James found himself tossing and turning in his bed, sleep eluding him like a wisp of smoke just beyond his grasp. The anticipation of Lady Olivia's arrival churned a tumult of thoughts and emotions within him, a maelstrom of hope and uncertainty that kept him staring at the shadows dancing across the ceiling.

What could he expect from this new governess or companion? A woman who, according to Alexander, possessed a brilliance and a willingness to embrace the challenge of educating Charlotte. The prospect of change, of a fresh start, was both exhilarating and daunting, and James couldn't shake the nagging doubt that lingered at the back of his mind.

As the hours crept by, James replayed the conversation with Alexander in his head, dissecting every detail, every word. What were her motivations, her methods? Would she truly connect with Charlotte in a way that previous governesses had not? The weight of responsibility pressed heavily upon him, the desire to provide the best for his daughter battling with the fear of yet another disappointment. The uncertainty was a bitter companion, feeding his restlessness, keeping sleep just out of reach.

Eventually, the first light of dawn seeped through the curtains, casting a soft glow on the room's familiar furnishings. James let out a weary sigh, resigning himself to the fact that the night's rest would remain elusive. Today would be a day of new beginnings, of introductions and first impressions. He needed to be ready, to present a calm and collected front, even as the storm of his own doubts raged on within. With a final glance at the slowly brightening sky, James rose from his bed, determined to face the day and whatever it might bring.

His valet began the familiar routine of dressing for the day. He chose a well-tailored dark blue coat that complemented his stature and a crisp white shirt that spoke of quiet elegance. He hadn't exactly maintained sartorial elegance while ensconced at the estate, but he wanted to convey both the seriousness of his position as the Duke of Wallingford and the warmth of a father dedicated to his daughter's well-being. He hadn't been this nervous about a new governess for Charlotte before. Then again, he'd never felt this desperate before.

With his attire in order, James took a moment to gather his thoughts. He stood before a portrait of his late wife, her gentle smile captured in the soft brushstrokes, a reminder of the love and partnership that had once filled these halls. James sent a silent prayer to her. He hoped that everything would go perfectly, that Lady Olivia would see the sincerity in their need and agree to stay. The thought of finding a governess who could truly connect with Charlotte, who could bring a sense of stability and joy to their lives, was a beacon of hope in the lingering shadow of Elizabeth's absence.

As he turned away from the portrait, James felt a renewed sense of determination. He straightened his cravat, took a deep breath, and stepped out of his room, ready to face whatever challenges and opportunities the arrival of Lady Olivia might bring.

The morning of Olivia's departure dawned bright and clear, the sun casting a soft, golden glow over the Weston estate. Amidst the flurry of last-minute preparations, Olivia found a moment to say goodbye to her sisters and Alexander. The farewells were bittersweet, filled with tight hugs and promises to write often.

Caroline spoke excitedly about Olivia's new adventure, while Mary, with a hint of sadness in her eyes, clung to Olivia a moment longer than usual.

Alexander offered a reassuring smile and a firm handshake, his demeanour confident.

As Olivia stepped away from her family, she felt a surge of emotions —gratitude for their support, sadness at the parting, and a growing sense of anticipation for what lay ahead.

The journey to the Duke of Wallingford's estate was to be made by carriage, a sturdy, comfortable vehicle drawn by a pair of strong horses. As the carriage rolled away from the Weston estate, Olivia settled into the plush seat, the rhythmic trot of the horses and the gentle rocking of the carriage lulling her into a reflective silence.

Jane took out the book she was reading. Moral Tales for Young People by Maria Edgeworth. Olivia found the moralising tone patronising, but Jane loved it, and there was no doubt its easy language and grammar helped her to slowly read.

The scenery unfolded before her, the urban landscape of her familiar world gradually giving way to the open countryside, where fields of green stretched to the horizon and the air carried the scent of earth and growth. The transition from the city's structured elegance to the country's wild beauty was both striking and soothing, and Olivia found herself captivated by the changing views outside her window.

As the miles passed, Olivia's thoughts turned to her family, whom would miss more than she had anticipated. The laughter shared at the dinner table, the quiet moments of companionship, even the occasional squabbles, all took on a new significance in the face of her departure. The comfort of their presence, once taken for granted, now felt like a luxury she had left behind. Yet, despite the pang of longing, Olivia couldn't deny the excitement that bubbled within her at the thought of the new adventure awaiting her. The opportunity to make a difference in a child's life, to step into a role that challenged and intrigued her, was a prospect too enticing to ignore.

As the carriage navigated the winding country roads, she contemplated the upcoming meeting with the duke and his daughter, wondering about the personalities and challenges that awaited her. The unknowns of the situation—the state of the estate, the temperament of the child she was to tutor, and how she would be received by the duke himself—swirled in her mind, a mix of apprehension and eager anticipation.

When the carriage finally slowed, signalling its approach to the Wallingford estate, Olivia took a deep breath, steeling herself for the moment of arrival. The gates opened to reveal a sweeping drive that led to a grand manor house, its impressive facade a testament to the family's history and stature. The footman who had travelled with her handed both herself and Jane out of the carriage, and she took a moment to absorb the beauty of her new surroundings, the vast gardens and the stately home that would be her world for the foreseeable future.

A wave of nervous excitement washed over her. The journey had taken a few hours, giving her ample time to ponder and fret over the unknowns that lay ahead. She took in a deep, steadying breath, the mix of anticipation and apprehension that comes with stepping into uncharted territory tightening her chest.

In that instant, standing on the threshold of a new beginning, a resolve settled within her. She was ready for this challenge, ready to embrace the adventure, and determined to make a positive impact in the lives of those she was about to meet.

The manor's size and opulence rivalled that of Alexander's estate, a comparison that did not escape Olivia. She was momentarily taken aback by the luxury before her, having known the comforts of a well-to-do life but never the extravagant display of wealth that the manor represented. The meticulously maintained gardens that surrounded the estate added to its majesty, with expanses of green lawns stretching out in every direction, bordered by neatly trimmed hedges and vibrant flower beds. It was a place where nature and luxury intertwined, creating a setting that was at once awe-inspiring and welcoming.

She found herself drawn to the beauty and tranquillity of her surroundings.

"I hope it's as grand on the inside as it is on the outside," Jane whispered.

Olivia didn't answer as the door swung open to reveal two men who bowed politely and ran to get her bags from the coach.

The butler invited her inside. Without a second thought, she handed him her pelisse and stepped across the threshold, her attention immediately captured by the grandeur of the interior.

"I believe the duke is expecting me." Olivia spoke to no one in particular.

Her gaze had already shifted, her attention caught by the splendour within. "Oh, look at that painting!" She moved closer to admire the artwork, her words overlapping any attempt by the man to speak.

He cleared his throat, trying again. "Actually, I—"

But Olivia's focus shifted anew, this time to a collection of books on a nearby table.

"These volumes! Are they first editions?" Finally, she turned back to him. "And where might I find the duke?" She had expected to be greeted by the household staff, maybe the housekeeper, not left wandering the entrance with only a silent stranger for company.

The man met her gaze with a flat look, the corners of his mouth twitching slightly in amusement at the situation. "I am the Duke of Wallingford."

Olivia took in the man before her, impeccably dressed and rather more handsome than she expected. He was striking to look at, with a strong jawline, deep-set eyes, and an air of quiet strength about him. She glanced behind him and caught the bland expression of the butler... the actual butler.

Her expression flickered with surprise then embarrassment, as she realized her mistake. She hadn't heard the man arrive, and had assumed she'd handed her coat to the butler, but it was the Duke of Wallingford himself standing before her with her coat still in hand.

Her cheeks heated to boiling point. No doubt she had flushed a deep shade of crimson as she absorbed the revelation. "I'm terribly sorry," she stammered, her embarrassment evident. She dropped into a courtesy. "Forgive me your Grace. I wasn't expecting... I didn't see—"

"No need for apologies. I should have waited in the drawing room until Debbit delivered you to me." He offered her a reassuring smile, seemingly unfazed by the mix-up, though the quirked brow suggested he found her lacking as a possible governess/companion and it didn't help assuage her insecurity.

She almost wished she was Ellie, who knew how to handle a scenario like this.

His voice was calm and measured, conveying a sense of casual ease that contrasted with the grandeur of his title and estate. "May I show you to your rooms and allow you to settle in?" His tone was polite and welcoming as he gracefully changed the subject. It was a gesture of hospitality, offering her a moment to regain her composure and acclimate to the unexpected dynamics of her new environment.

"That will be much appreciated. Thank you." Olivia's voice was steadier now, despite the whirlwind of emotions she had experienced upon her arrival. She was grateful for the chance to retreat and collect her thoughts after the whirlwind introduction.

As Jane and her followed the duke through the manor, Olivia marvelled at the turn her life had taken, leading her to this moment, to this place, and to the start of what promised to be a most intriguing chapter. Assuming he didn't send her back to Alexander after the embarrassing introduction, that is.

"Jane, the housekeeper will show you to your room," The Duke said, gesturing towards a larger woman, standing beside the butler.

"Thank you, Your Grace." Jane bobbed a low curtsey and went with the housekeeper.

"This way."

As they made their way through the elegant hallways of the manor, he began to outline the routine of the house and his expectations regarding Olivia's role as his daughter's governess. "The mornings are typically reserved for lessons." His voice echoed slightly off the high ceilings. "I would like for Charlotte to have a structured schedule, focusing on her studies before lunch. The afternoons can be more flexible, allowing for outdoor activities and practical learning experiences."

Olivia listened intently, nodding as she absorbed the information. The structure sounded reasonable, and she was already considering ways to make the lessons engaging for Charlotte.

Curiosity got the better of her. "When may I meet your daughter?"

"She'll be ready by supper time." James glanced at her, a thoughtful look crossing his features. "Charlotte can be a bit shy with new people, so I thought it best to give her some time to adjust to the idea of meeting you."

Continuing their tour, James led Olivia to her room. The door opened to reveal a spacious chamber bathed in natural light, with a large window offering views of the estate's sprawling gardens. The room was beautifully furnished, combining comfort with a simple elegance that made Olivia feel immediately at ease. As she took in her new surroundings, she felt a mix of gratitude and determination.

Before leaving Olivia to settle into her new quarters, James paused at the doorway, turning back to face her. "Is there anything else you need?"

Caught momentarily off guard by the question, Olivia remembered the coat still in his possession. With a slight blush heating her cheeks, she reached out to take the coat from him. "Thank you, your Grace." Her gratitude mixed with a touch of embarrassment for having forgotten about it until now.

James offered a slight nod, the corners of his mouth turning up in a small smile. "We dine at six to suit Charlotte as she enjoys dining with adults rather than alone in the nursery." He held her gaze, setting a clear expectation for their evening routine. No doubt he was aware of how unusual it was for parents to welcome their children to the dining table.

Did he expect her to recoil at the idea? She couldn't imagine being an only child and spending countless hours alone in the schoolroom or nursery. He was still waiting for a response from her.

"Thank you, Your Grace." Olivia curtsied slightly, acknowledging both his position as the duke and her role within his home. "The structure of the household seems orderly, respectful, and considerate. I appreciate your clarity in these matters."

He acknowledged her gesture with a nod, then turned and left, closing the door softly behind him. Olivia stood alone in her room, the silence settling around her like a cloak. The reality of her new life at the manor, with its routines and expectations, began to truly sink in. She was here on a mission of sorts, to educate and befriend Charlotte, and perhaps in doing so, find a place where she belonged. The thought was both daunting and exhilarating, a challenge she was now ready to face.

Chapter Six

The duke marched Charlotte down the corridor, his frustration palpable, embarrassment at her behaviour evident in every tense line of his body.

Upon encountering a maid—with no regard for what task she was currently engaged in—he barked out an order, his voice sharp with authority. "Start a bath for Charlotte, immediately."

The maid dropped a bundle of linen on the floor and scurried away, while Charlotte trailed behind him, her earlier defiance replaced with a sullen silence.

In her bedroom, James turned to his daughter, his shoulders tight, eyes narrowed. "Charlotte, look at you." He gestured to her dishevelled appearance. "You know how important today is, and yet you don't seem to care. I can hardly express my disappointment in your behaviour." His words were stern, but he didn't bother to check the underlying note of hurt, a father's pain at feeling disregarded by his child.

Charlotte shifted from one foot to the other. Her gaze fixed on the floor, her earlier bravado fading in the face of his reprimand.

James continued, his voice softer but no less firm. "I'm not asking you to change who you are, but there are times when we must present our best selves. Today, with Miss Darrow's arrival, was one of those

"

times. First impressions matter a great deal, and you arrive at super looking like a street urchin?"

He crouched down to her level, lifted her chin, and met her eyes with a sincerity that he hoped would reach her. "I need you to understand, Charlotte, that your actions reflect on our family. More importantly, they impact the relationships we have with those who come into our lives. Lady Olivia is here to help you, to teach you, and it's crucial that you give her—and yourself—a chance."

Charlotte's eyes, usually so bright with mischief, seemed to dim with the weight of his words. James placed a gentle hand on her shoulder, hoping to bridge the gap his sternness had created. "I know you're better than this." He softened his tone. "Let's show Lady Olivia the wonderful girl I know you are." In that moment, James' frustration was tempered by a father's love and hope. A silent plea for his daughter, young though she was, to rise to the occasion and embrace the opportunity before her.

James left Charlotte in the capable hands of her nanny, trusting that she would be properly prepared for supper. With a heavy heart, he made his way to the drawing room, where he found Olivia seated and engrossed in a book. She didn't look up as he entered, seemingly unaware of his presence.

He took a moment to observe her. She'd changed into a dinner dress of lavender and soft ivory, a delicate silk shawl over her shoulders. Lady Olivia was undeniably attractive. Her dark hair fell in soft waves around her face, framing her features with a natural elegance. Her eyes, a striking shade of blue, were focused intently on the pages before her, a testament to her love for literature. The freckles that dotted her cheeks added a touch of youthful charm, giving her a warm, approachable appearance. It was a pleasant surprise to find that his new governess was not only capable and intelligent but also possessed a quiet beauty that was both understated and captivating.

A pang of guilt struck him as he continued to study her. It was inappropriate, he chided himself, to notice such things about a woman in her professional capacity, especially one employed in his household. With a mental shake, he banished the thoughts, reminding himself of the boundaries that must be maintained between them. Clearing his throat to announce his presence, he prepared to join her for supper, determined to keep their interactions strictly professional.

Olivia glanced up, her attention shifting from the book to him. A pretty blush touched her cheeks, perhaps from being caught unawares or from the sudden shift in focus. She closed her book with a soft thud and offered him a polite smile as he took a seat on the opposite sofa.

"Lady Olivia, I must apologize for Charlotte's behaviour this evening." James crossed his legs, he felt rather like a schoolboy trying to explain an unsatisfactory test result to his father.

Olivia waved away his apology with a graceful hand. "It's quite all right, Your Grace," she assured him, her tone understanding. "I'm familiar with the testing behaviour children exhibit when meeting someone new."

"Are you?" Scepticism threaded through his voice. It was hard to believe that someone as composed and seemingly gentle as Olivia could handle the whirlwind that was Charlotte.

She opened her mouth to respond, perhaps to offer him some insight into her experience or reassure him further, but just then, Debbit arrived and announced that Miss Charlotte would be down shortly, and that dinner was served.

Olivia closed her mouth and stood. James, ever the gentleman held out his arm to take her into the dining room.

James regretted the interruption. It had felt like Olivia was about to tell him something important that might have given him a better understanding of how she intended to approach her role as Charlotte's governess. But the moment had passed, and he couldn't think of a way to reopen the conversation.

The table was set with an array of dishes that showcased the cook's culinary prowess. A platter of roasted chicken, its skin golden and crisp, sat alongside a bowl of steamed vegetables, vibrant and fresh from the manor's gardens. There were also potatoes, mashed to rich and creamy perfection, and a gravy boat filled with rich, savoury sauce. A basket of warm, crusty bread completed the meal, the aroma of freshly baked dough wafting through the air. A simple enough spread as he was used to eating with Charlotte.

As they waited for Charlotte to join them, an awkward silence settled between James and Olivia. The earlier ease with which they had conversed was replaced by a palpable tension, as if the interruption had erected a barrier between them. James found himself stealing glances at Olivia, noting the way she fiddled with the fork and took dainty sips of wine. He was acutely aware of her presence, the graceful movements, and the soft sound of her breathing, all of which seemed amplified in the quiet of the room.

The air between them was charged with unspoken words and unsolved mysteries, a tension that was both uncomfortable and intriguing. What thoughts were running through her mind? What questions did she have about her place here? He'd invited her to join himself and Charlotte at meals as naturally as if she were a member of the family or a close family friend. Of course, Alexander was a capital fellow, and he was charged with Olivia's well-being, which meant that James was now the one so charged.

The silence stretched on until Charlotte entered the dining room, a model of propriety, her appearance transformed from the dishevelled state he'd found her in. She was clean and properly dressed, her hair neatly combed and her attire fitting. However, the frown on her face was a clear indication that she was not pleased with her earlier rebuke. She took a seat across from Olivia, her movements deliberate as she began to plate her food without a word of greeting.

"Charlotte, what do we say when we join others at the table?" James chided gently, hoping to remind her of the basic courtesies expected of her.

Charlotte's frown deepened, and for a moment, it looked as though she was going to argue or ignore the prompt altogether. But then, after a brief pause, she relented, her voice strained as she forced the words out as she nodded first at Olivia and then James. "I do apologize. Forgive me. Lady Darrow, Father."

The apology was clearly begrudging. James heaved a heavy sigh. What was he to do with her? Olivia's silence heightened the tension across his shoulders. The clinking of silverware against plates and the occasional sound of a chair shifting were the only noises that punctuated the quiet. He glanced between his Miss Charlotte and Lady Olivia. Surely, she wasn't crying craven this early. But so far, he'd seen no sign of a spirit to match to demonstrate his new governess could handle his daughter's stubbornness.

Olivia concentrated on her meal, each bite deliberate and thoughtful. She seemed acutely aware of the tense atmosphere, casting occasional, discreet glances at Charlotte. It was as though she were trying to discern the young girl's mood, searching for any hint that might help her penetrate the barriers Charlotte had erected around herself. He watched, hopeful. The silence hung between them like a challenge, a puzzle awaiting resolution. Suddenly, he felt a palpable shift in the air—Olivia's resolve to forge a connection with her charge was almost tangible, her determination quietly asserting itself in the quiet of the room.

Charlotte, on the other hand, ate quietly, her earlier defiance replaced with a sullen compliance. She kept her eyes on her plate, avoiding eye contact with both her father and Olivia. The forced apology had taken something out of her, a small surrender in the ongoing battle of wills.

As the servants cleared away Charlotte's plate, her gaze landed on Olivia's book.

He hadn't noticed that she'd carried it with her to the table. A testament to his focus on this first meeting between them all.

"You're not allowed to have a book at the table, Miss Olivia." She pointed at the offending volume, her tone accusatory.

James corrected her. "You know well enough to address your new governess as Lady Olivia, not Olivia, nor Miss Darrow."

Unperturbed, Charlotte continued, "Well, Miss Lady Darrow has a book at the table, and you should be lecturing her because it's against the rules."

James glanced at Olivia, expecting her to be taken aback by Charlotte's boldness. Instead, he found her eyes sparkling with humour.

"Do you like to read?" Olivia ignored the accusation.

"Yes, but no one lets me read what I want." Charlotte folded her arms across her chest, her frustration evident. It was an argument they'd suffered with every governess Charlotte had worked her way through so far.

"Well, you are right to point out that I shouldn't have brought the book to the table. I won't do it again. But I'd like to know what you want to read that has been forbidden to you?" Olivia inquired.

Charlotte's eyes lit up with passion. "They make me read boring primers and stuffy history when all I want is to read about elves and dwarves and princesses and far off places—"

"Charlotte." James interjected, but Olivia cut him off.

"I'm happy to share a book like that." Olivia said, her voice warm and encouraging. "But your previous governesses were quite right to insist you read about history, geography and so on, regardless of how stuffy it is."

"What book will you share?" Charlotte conveniently ignored anything further about books she deemed stuffy.

"There are important lessons in our history that we should apply to our present." Olivia paused, then offered a compromise that took James by surprise. "I have a suggestion. I will revisit the lesson plan to ensure it meets your aptitude rather than your age, and provided you apply yourself to your lessons and behave well in class, I'll read to you from my book each night before bed."

James started to protest, "You don't have to—"

But Charlotte interrupted him. "What book? If it's a good one then, I'll do it."

"I am thinking of 'Gulliver's Travels."

Charlotte's face lit up. "Mrs. Rutherford said that story is totally unsuitable for children."

Olivia shrugged. "It is, of course, full of adventure and fantastical tales of Gulliver's voyages to imaginary lands. But I have never found it unsuitable. Indeed, I read it to both my sisters when they were quite young."

"I will be very good." Charlotte grinned.

James had no doubt she was planning something wicked to keep Olivia on her toes.

Olivia nodded in approval. "Now that you've finished your supper, why don't you see your nanny and get ready for bed? I shall be up shortly to read from the first chapter."

"We can start tonight?" Charlotte asked, her voice filled with hopeful anticipation.

"As long as your father allows it." Olivia turned her gaze to James, seeking his permission.

James considered the arrangement for a moment before responding. "Only if you retire without a fuss."

"I will." Charlotte's demeanour had brightened at the prospect. She stood up, her smile genuine for the first time that evening, and politely asked, "May I be excused?"

James hid his surprise at his daughter's sudden transformation. "You may."

A sense of relief washed over him. Perhaps, just perhaps, Lady Olivia was exactly what Charlotte needed.

Chapter Seven

Charlotte closed the door behind her, and James thanked Olivia with an enthusiasm probably beyond that required.

Olivia shook her head modestly. "My role requires that I build up trust between Charlotte and myself. It's of great import to do so. I understand the responsibility I've taken on and am committed to fulfilling it."

She stood, gathering her book with a graceful motion. "Thank you for the opportunity to do so, Your Grace." Her gaze met James' for a moment before she turned to leave the room.

As she walked back to her room, Olivia could still feel the weight of the duke's gaze, both unsettling and reassuring. Though why did he have to be so handsome, and so obviously devoted to his daughter? She would need to maintain a delicate balance in her new role. She was determined to prove herself capable, not just for Charlotte's sake, but for her own sense of purpose and fulfilment.

It hadn't been as uncomfortable as she'd expected. In fact, she'd been treated more like a guest than a governess. More like the companion that Alexander had mentioned to her when they first spoke about Charlotte. She grinned to herself imaging all the ways the child had outfoxed her previous governesses.

Olivia closed her bedroom door softly behind her, the silence of the space a stark contrast to the lively atmosphere of her family home. She changed from her dinner gown into a comfortable wrapper for the evening. A pang of homesickness speared her chest. She already missed the familiar sounds of her sisters running down the hall, their laughter and chatter filling the air. She longed for the banter between Alexander and Eleanor, the warmth of their companionship, and the sense of belonging that came with being surrounded by her loved ones.

She shook herself free of the notion. Her place was here, in this grand manor, with a young girl who needed her guidance. A conviction that she could make a difference in Charlotte's life filled her. She may prove to be a challenging young lady, and perhaps some of the days ahead would be daunting, but Olivia would face them with patience, understanding, and a steadfast commitment to her new charge.

The quiet of her room was a reminder of the distance from her family, but it also offered a space for contemplation and growth. She was here to help Charlotte navigate the complexities of growing up, to provide her with the tools she needed to thrive. She searched through her bag until she found her beautifully illustrated and finely bound copy of Gulliver's Travels.

Olivia stepped from her room with the book in hand and comfortable slippers on her feet. Along the way, she bumped into Charlotte's maid, who gave her a quick nod and muttered, "Good luck" before scurrying off.

Olivia gazed after her with a shaking head. What challenges awaited her?

She tapped gently on Charlotte's door and stepped inside to find the young girl perched at the foot of her bed. Charlotte's hair was now twisted and lay in unruly tangles on her shoulders. No doubt the maid had tried to braid the hair and Charlotte had objected.

"Please bring me your hairbrush." Olivia's experience with her younger sisters would come in useful. She kept her tone kind yet resolute.

"Why?" Charlotte countered, her arms crossed, and expression tinged with defiance.

Olivia offered a mild reprimand softened by the warmth in her voice. "It's good to ask questions, Charlotte, but try to ask them nicely. Bring me the brush, and I'll explain why it's important to take care of your long tresses."

Charlotte hesitated for a moment, weighing Olivia's words, then hopped off the bed with a sigh. She retrieved the hairbrush from her dressing table and handed it to Olivia. As she did, her eyes were curious, softened from their earlier hardness.

Olivia took the brush, smiling reassuringly. "Turn around. Sit right here, on my lap."

Charlotte did as she was told. "What are you doing?"

"Let's tame these tangles." Olivia began to gently work the brush through Charlotte's hair. "Taking care of your hair reflects how you care for yourself, and it's a moment to think and reflect."

"Connie pulls my hair." Charlotte pouted.

"Do you wriggle and fuss?"

Charlotte stayed silent, an admission of sorts, Olivia gathered. It was lucky she could tempt her into obedience with a story.

"I'm going to help you get ready for bed properly." Olivia said. "And then I'll read to you."

"You'll still read to me?" Charlotte asked, her voice softer now.

"Of course, I will," Olivia assured her. "I told you I would, did I not?"

"Yes, but many people promise things, but not everyone delivers," Charlotte admitted, her voice tinged with vulnerability beneath her usual bravado.

"Well, I'm someone who keeps her promises."

"My mother used to do this every night when I was a child." Olivia said as she continued to brush Charlotte's hair, the rhythmic strokes brought back a flood of memories. A wistful sadness tugged at her heart. "It was our special time together. She'd tell me stories, or we'd talk about our day. It always quieted my mind and helped me prepare for bed. Made me feel loved and safe."

Charlotte, looked up at Olivia with wide eyes. "Does your mama still do it?"

The question hit Olivia like a physical blow, and for a moment, she had to fight to keep her composure. She thought of her mother, once so vibrant and full of life, now confined to her bed, her once-strong hands now frail and weak.

"No." Olivia's voice caught in her throat as she fought back tears. "She can't anymore." She quickly blinked away the moisture in her eyes, not wanting to burden Charlotte with her own sadness.

Though the sense of loss was profound, not just for the physical presence of her mother, but also for the comforting rituals and the sense of normalcy that had vanished from her life. Yet, there was also a glimmer of solace in being able to provide the same comfort to Charlotte, a similar moment of peace and connection.

Olivia finished brushing Charlotte's hair, each stroke smoother than the last as the tangles gave way to soft, flowing locks. The child relaxed under her gentle ministrations, the earlier tension slowly dissipating. Once satisfied that her hair was neatly brushed, Olivia set the brush aside and neatly braided Charlotte's hair.

She helped the girl up and guided her to the head of the bed. "Lie down now."

Charlotte complied, slipping under the covers. Olivia took a moment to tuck the blankets snugly around her, ensuring she was warm and comfortable. The act was simple, yet it carried a weight of care and protection, a silent promise of safety in the night.

As she straightened up, Olivia caught a glimpse of Charlotte's face, now calm and vulnerable in the soft glow of the bedside lamp. It was a stark contrast to the defiant, spirited girl she had encountered earlier in the evening. This glimpse of the child beneath the bravado reinforced Olivia's resolve to help her grew stronger.

"Are you ready for your story?" Olivia invited Charlotte into the world of imagination and adventure that awaited them.

Charlotte nodded, a spark of excitement lighting up her eyes, a reminder of the magic that stories held for her.

Olivia opened the book and began to read,

"My father had a small estate in Nottinghamshire; I was the third of five sons. He sent me to Emmanuel College in Cambridge at fourteen years old, where I resided three years, and applied myself close to my studies..."

The narrative quickly moved to Gulliver's first voyage to the East Indies. But as Olivia read, Charlotte's eyelids grow heavy, the words carrying her off to a land of dreams and wonder. When she was sure Charlotte was asleep, Olivia closed the book and placed it on the nightstand. She blew out the candle and whispered a goodnight to the sleeping child.

A sense of accomplishment and hope for the journey ahead filled her as she quietly left the room.

But as she shut the door behind her, she was startled to find James standing just outside, his presence unexpected. He seemed to be caught off guard as well, looking away almost awkwardly as their eyes met.

"Is everything all right, Your Grace?"

"Indeed, I am sure it is." His voice betrayed a hint of unease. "James, if you would."

She cleared her throat, the shift in dynamics momentarily disconcerting. "James," she said, trying out the familiarity of his given name. "Then of course you must call me Olivia."

His eyes darkened slightly at the sound of his name on her lips, a subtle change that Olivia couldn't quite interpret. After a brief pause, he nodded. "Thank you, Olivia. Let me walk you to your room."

Surely, he hadn't been waiting just to walk her the short trip to her room. Perhaps he'd listened outside the door to check that she had indeed read to his daughter. Curiosity filled her, sensing undercurrents of emotion in him. Undercurrents he kept under tight control.

As they walked together down the dimly lit corridor, the silence of the night enveloping them, Olivia was acutely aware of James' presence beside her. Their shoulders brushed occasionally, a fleeting touch that sent a ripple of awareness through her. He was tall, his height accentuated by the straightness of his posture and the confident, measured steps he took. Each brush of their shoulders was a reminder of the physical contrast between them, yet it also served to highlight a growing sense of familiarity and ease in each other's company.

The subtle contact was unintentional, yet it carried a weight of unspoken communication. It was as if, in that brief contact, they acknowledged the shared experience of the evening, the challenges, and the small victories. Olivia stole glances at James, noting the strong line of his jaw and the way his hair fell just so, catching glimpses of the man beyond the title of Duke. There was a complexity to him that intrigued her. A depth she had only begun to perceive.

The walk to her room seemed shorter than Olivia had anticipated, the quiet companionship making the time pass quickly. As they reached her door, she turned to face him, the proximity bringing a heightened awareness of his stature and the quiet strength he exuded.

"Thank you for escorting me." Olivia was about to step into her room when James reached out, his fingers lightly grasping her elbow.

The moment his touch registered, he immediately withdrew his hand, as if the contact had burned him. The suddenness of the gesture caught Olivia off guard, her heart skipping a beat at the unexpected intimacy.

"Thank you for coming on such short notice. You are the first that she has taken to so quickly." James spoke in a steady measure, but his eyes betrayed a hint of inner turmoil. "I look forward to hearing about your lessons and progress." His words were formal, yet there was an underlying sincerity that resonated with Olivia.

She nodded, her mind a whirl of thoughts and emotions. "Of course. Goodnight Your Grace." She quickly stepped into her room, closing the door softly behind her.

Leaning against it, she hoped he couldn't hear the racing of her heart, that he hadn't noticed the flutter of excitement that must have shown on her face. Hopefully the hallway had been dark enough to keep her emotions well hidden.

Olivia made her way to the desk by the window, the events of the evening still replaying in her mind. She knew that sleep would elude her now, her thoughts too active, too filled with the possibilities and challenges of the days ahead. She moved to the desk and pulled out a fresh sheet of paper and dipped her pen in ink, ready to outline the curriculum she planned to begin with Charlotte.

As she wrote, her mind buzzed with ideas, Charlotte seemed advanced in her literacy skills, but she needed to make sure she truly had a solid grasp of the basics of reading and writing. It was easy to come up with more creative endeavours to engage Charlotte's imagination. She thought about incorporating stories of elves and dwarves, of princesses and far-off places, into their lessons, weaving a tapestry of learning that was both educational and captivating. She had to strike a balance in order to keep Charlotte's spirited nature in mind while instilling the discipline necessary for her education.

The clock ticked away the hours as Olivia worked. She was determined to make a difference in Charlotte's life. To be the governess that James hoped for and the mentor that Charlotte needed.

As the night deepened, Olivia finally set aside her pen, her plans for the curriculum taking shape. She yawned and fell into bed almost asleep. The road ahead would be challenging, but she was ready to face it with determination and a heart full of hope.

Chapter Eight

The yellow of a rising sun filtered through the curtains of his study. Papers and reports on his desk forgotten, James found himself unusually preoccupied with anticipation for how the day would unfold for his daughter and her new governess. He was curious, almost eager to see if Lady Olivia's—Olivia's—unconventional approach would yield any positive changes in Charlotte's behaviour.

But James could not linger at home to witness the lessons firsthand. His attention was needed elsewhere. His steward had an agricultural improvement for him to approve, and a group of tenants had requested a meeting with him. Then he'd have to hasten to attend a meeting to discuss proposed corn tariffs followed by another meeting with local dignitaries to discuss a proposed visit by the Prince Regent. He would be lucky to make it back in time for dinner with Charlotte. And Olivia, of course.

As he prepared to leave, James sent up a prayer that the tentative connection he'd observed forming between Charlotte and Olivia held and grew in strength. He hadn't meant to listen outside his daughter's door last night. His feet had carried him there of their own accord, and then he lurked like a nosy footman. He was glad he had though. Olivia had a determination and warmth about her that he hadn't seen in any of the previous governesses.

There was something about her that made him hope, perhaps foolishly, that she might be the one to finally reach his headstrong daughter.

As he left the house, early morning light danced across the gardens. Would Olivia take Charlotte outside for some of their lessons? Would she succeed in finding a way to make learning enjoyable for a girl who had always resisted the confines of traditional education. He fervently hoped so. For his own sake as much as Charlotte's, he prayed for laughter and lightness in a home that had been weighed down by too much seriousness for far too long.

With a final sigh, James strode to his waiting carriage and steeled himself for the day ahead. He had to trust Olivia to handle Charlotte's learning. The morning had barely started and yet he could hardly wait to inquire about the day's events upon his return. For the first time in a long while, he was genuinely interested in what the answer might be.

After approving the new process and meeting with his tenants, the duke hurried to his office in town. Edward, his secretary, met him with files for the meeting schedule and paperwork for upcoming court cases for assessment. It made for a busy day.

As the hours passed, James found himself occasionally glancing at the clock, his thoughts drifting back to the ongoing lessons between Charlotte and Olivia. Were they getting along? Was Charlotte interested and showing signs of improvement in her behaviour? There was something about Lady Olivia that caught his attention, something that made him believe that change was possible, not just for Charlotte, but perhaps for himself as well.

James returned to Wallingford House from a long day of work expecting to see Olivia and Charlotte in the drawing room awaiting his presence before starting dinner. But the drawing room was empty. So was the dining room.

"Where are they, Debbit?"

"I believe Lady Olivia took Miss Charlotte into the gardens, Your Grace."

James grunted a response. The sun was already low in the sky, and neither lady had any business being in the gardens at this time. But he marched to the terrace doors to find the pair.

He stepped outside into the fading light of the day. A trail of dirt led into the gardens, the sound of laughter coming from his dear Elizabeth's favourite rose garden.

Rounding a corner, he caught sight of Olivia and Charlotte crouched down, the hems of their gowns streaked with dirt, near the flower beds that his late wife had cherished. The sight of them, so carefree and dirty amidst the carefully tended blooms, ignited a fury within him.

"What on earth are you doing?" his voice boomed across the garden.

Olivia stood, her face flushed. Who knew whether it was from the cooling air, the laughter, or the sudden reprimand.

"We are having a lesson about the different flowers all within the rose family—" Olivia tried to explain, her voice calm despite the rising tension.

But James was beyond listening. The sight of the mud, the laughter, the blatant disregard for the sanctity of Elizabeth's garden were too much.

"This is unacceptable," he interrupted Olivia. "I knew this was too good to be true." He didn't try to hide the disappointment in his voice, or the frustration in his clenched fists. He had hoped for so much, only to be let down once again.

"You're relieved of your position, Lady Olivia. I'll have my carriage return you home tomorrow." His heart was heavy with the decision, but he saw no other choice.

He stormed back inside, pangs of sorrow piercing his chest. He had hoped for a change, for a new beginning. But now, with his dear wife's garden disturbed and the laughter still echoing in his ears, he felt only the familiar weight of disappointment. It was a setback, another in a long line of them, and he wondered if things would ever truly change for the better.

"Excuse me?" Olivia tugged on his arm. Disbelief was etched across her face. "You dismiss me after just one day—"

"I hired you to teach my daughter. Not frolic in the mud with her." He spun to face her, his expression a flash of anger. "How is this teaching her to fulfil the role of Lady Charlotte, or teaching her mind, or engaging her interest?"

"I am doing exactly as you asked." Olivia pointed her finger at his chest, her jaw stiff. "We are learning about the flowers. How different they can be while so similar in so many ways."

"My wife planted those flowers." James responded through clenched teeth, his emotions raw. He stepped back, desperate to get away from her. Away from his own anger.

"You mean, Charlotte's mother, the Duchess of Wallingford?" Olivia closed the distance between them. "Charlotte asked to visit that garden in particular. She wants to be close to her, to learn more about the kind of woman she was, but you shut her down. You protect her mother's spirit with a reverence that is admirable, but Charlotte does not feel close to her, and does not know her the way she wants to. And this creates a distance between you and Charlotte because you are keeping her from understanding her own mother."

"You have some nerve." James narrowed his gaze. "How dare you make such assumptions."

"It's clear, if you would just look," Olivia countered, her voice steady despite the tension. "You see your daughter as spirited and that's all. You don't realize the nuances that make her your daughter. She's more than just fierce and loud and passionate. She's scared. She's curious. Charlotte is desperate for a connection that you don't permit her to have because you shutter her away here and shutter out her mother's presence instead of allowing her to explore, to learn, to seek out answers to questions."

The confrontation hung heavy in the air, a clash of wills and perspectives that left them both reeling, each grappling with the truths and accusations that had been laid bare.

As the heated exchange between them simmered down, James found his gaze lingering on Olivia. Despite the anger and frustration that had fuelled their dispute, he couldn't deny the attraction he felt towards her. Her passion, her conviction, and even her defiance stirred something within him that he hadn't anticipated. His eyes traced the contours of her face, admiring the fire in her eyes that spoke of her unwavering determination.

Unbidden, his gaze dropped to her lips, and a surprising realisation hit him—he wanted to kiss her. The thought jolted him, a rush of desire mingling with the remnants of his anger. It was a dangerous, reckless impulse, one that he knew he had no right to entertain. She was his employee. A woman who had just challenged him in a way no one else had dared, and yet the thought of tasting the defiance on her lips was tantalizing.

James forced himself to look away, to regain control over his wayward thoughts. He was the Duke of Wallingford, a man of discipline and responsibility, not one to be swayed by fleeting attractions. The intensity of the moment had clouded his judgment, but he knew he had to remain steadfast. He couldn't afford to let his personal feelings interfere with his duty as a father and as a duke. The line between them had to remain clear, no matter how much he found himself drawn to the spirited governess standing before him.

"If you want me to leave, I'll go." Olivia folded her hands at her waist. "But if I go, you must ascertain if you truly wish to help your daughter maintain her free-spirited nature without the ton's expectations smothering her. You don't realize you're suffocating her just as much as the rules of society."

James's jaw ticked at her words, a visible sign of his irritation. He couldn't deny the truth in her statement, but the defiant look in her eyes made him want to argue, to push back against her accusations. However, before he could respond, Charlotte's voice cut through the tension.

"Please, Father." Charlotte's eyes were wide. "Please don't send her away."

James stared at his dishevelled daughter, the sight of her standing up for Olivia stirring a mix of emotions within him.

"Clean yourself up for dinner, Charlotte. I expect you on your best behaviour."

He gave Olivia a curt nod. "Dinner in thirty minutes, Lady Olivia."

He spun away and headed inside, leaving Olivia and Charlotte behind. As he walked away, he tried to shake the thought of Olivia's lips from his mind.

But the memory lingered, a reminder of the complexities that had entangled his thoughts and emotions since her arrival.

Chapter Nine

After the confrontation in the garden, Olivia made her way back to her room, her mind racing with a whirlwind of emotions. She was furious with James, his accusations and dismissal stinging more than she cared to admit. As she freshened up, splashing cool water on her face, she tried to make sense of why his opinion mattered so much to her. She had come here to do a job, to nurture Charlotte's spirit as he had requested, and she was doing just that. And now he was upset with her? It hardly seemed fair.

The more she thought about it, the more frustrated she became. She had seen a side of Charlotte that James seemed blind to. A child yearning for a connection to her late mother, for a sense of freedom and understanding. Olivia had tried to provide that, to be the bridge between Charlotte and the world her father kept her sheltered from. Wasn't that what he wanted? Wasn't that the whole point of her being here?

As she paced her room, Olivia realized that her anger stemmed from more than just professional pride. She cared about Charlotte and wanted to make a real difference in her life. She cared about James's opinion, about gaining his trust and proving that she could handle the responsibility he had entrusted her with. It was a frustrating realization, one that left her feeling vulnerable and exposed.

Taking a deep breath, Olivia tried to calm her racing thoughts. She needed to stay focused, not letting her emotions get the best of her. She had a job to do, a child to teach and nurture. She couldn't afford to be distracted by her feelings and the turmoil that James Montgomery stirred within her. And most importantly, she had to persuade His Grace, the Duke of Wallingford, to allow her to stay.

Resolved to keep her composure, Olivia headed to dinner, determined to face whatever challenges lay ahead with grace and professionalism. She would prove to James that she was the right choice for Charlotte, that she could keep her spirit alive while still respecting the boundaries of her role. It was a delicate balance, but Olivia was ready to meet the challenge head-on.

When Olivia entered the dining room, she found James already seated at the table, engrossed in the evening paper. His sleeves were rolled up to his elbows, revealing strong forearms that spoke of a man accustomed to physical as well as intellectual pursuits. There was a casual elegance to his posture, a relaxed authority that was undeniably attractive. Olivia hated that she noticed these details, her eyes lingering on him longer than they should. It was a distraction she couldn't afford, especially now.

She quickly shook herself out of her reverie, chastising herself for letting her thoughts wander. This was not the time for such distractions. She needed to focus on her role, on Charlotte, and on navigating the complex dynamics of her position in the household. With a quiet resolve, she took her seat at the table, hoping that James hadn't noticed her momentary lapse.

As she settled into her chair, Olivia took a deep breath, mentally preparing herself for the meal ahead. She was determined to maintain her professionalism and keep her interactions with James strictly related to Charlotte's well-being and education. It was essential that she not let personal feelings interfere with her duties, no matter how challenging that might prove to be.

James glanced over at her, his gaze lingering for a moment longer than necessary. "You have," he began, gesturing vaguely at his own face.

Olivia frowned, confused. "What is it, Your Grace?"

James let out a huff of exasperation and leaned over, his hand reaching out to gently wipe away a smudge of dirt from her cheek. The unexpected touch caught Olivia off guard, his proximity suddenly much closer than she had anticipated. The feel of his hand on her face, the warmth of his skin against hers, were enough to send a rush of heat to her cheeks, leaving her flustered and more than a little embarrassed.

James' hand lingered on her cheek longer than necessary, his fingers lightly tracing the line of her jaw as if he were reluctant to pull away. Their eyes met, and Olivia found herself caught in his gaze, a silent communication passing between them that she couldn't quite decipher. His eyes, dark and intense, dropped to her lips, and without thinking, she ran her tongue over her bottom lip, a subconscious response to the tension that crackled in the air between them.

At her action, James's eyes widened slightly, a flicker of something unreadable passing through them. His grip on her face tightened just a fraction, a barely perceptible change that sent a shiver down Olivia's spine. The moment stretched out, charged with an unspoken energy that neither of them seemed able to break. Olivia's heart raced, her breaths coming a little quicker as she waited for his next move, unsure of what she wanted it to be.

Their moment of charged silence was abruptly shattered by Charlotte's presence, the young girl's voice cutting through the tension like a knife. James and Olivia broke away from each other quickly, as though they had been burned, both suddenly very aware of the impropriety of their closeness. The air between them, once thick with unspoken words and emotions, now felt awkward and charged with a different kind of energy—one of embarrassment and confusion. They both turned to face Charlotte, attempting to mask their discomfort with smiles that didn't quite reach their eyes.

During dinner, Charlotte was noticeably more sombre than usual. She went out of her way to use her manners, carefully placing her napkin on her lap and using her utensils with exaggerated precision. It was a stark contrast to her usual spirited demeanour. Had the earlier events in the garden affected her more than she let on at the time? Charlotte's efforts to behave impeccably seemed almost like a silent plea for approval. A way to make amends for the earlier transgressions.

Olivia, on the other hand, found herself in a different kind of struggle. She tried not to watch James during the meal, but she couldn't help it. Her eyes were drawn to him, noticing the way his jaw tensed when he was deep in thought and the slight curve of his lips when he found something amusing. Her awareness of his every movement was disturbing. She wished there was something to focus her attention on other than the man sitting across from her.

The tension from their earlier encounter lingered in the air, an unspoken undercurrent that neither of them addressed. Olivia found herself hyper-aware of the space between them and the crackling air whenever their eyes met. This attraction she felt towards him was unsettling, especially given the circumstances. She was here to educate Charlotte and be a stabilizing presence in the young girl's life, not to become entangled in whatever this was with James. She was not his equal in standing, nor as a member of his staff.

As dinner progressed, Olivia forced herself to focus on Charlotte, to engage her in conversation and praise her for her impeccable manners.

As the meal came to an end, Charlotte turned to her father, her eyes filled with moisture. "Please, Father, don't send Lady Olivia away." Her voice trembled. "I'll be good, I promise. I just really wanted to see Mother's garden before winter, and Miss Darrow said she could teach me how to keep the garden blooming beautifully." Tears started to form in her eyes, her emotions spilling over.

Olivia's heart ached for the young girl. James's expression softened as he glanced at his daughter, the resolve in his eyes giving way to understanding.

James glanced over at Olivia for a moment before enveloping Charlotte in a hug. "I'll discuss things with Lady Olivia. Now, get ready for bed."

Charlotte turned to Olivia, her eyes still glistening with tears. "Will you brush my hair again?" Hope filled her words. "And read me a chapter?"

Olivia looked to James for approval, and he nodded once, giving his consent.

"I will," Olivia promised Charlotte. "After I speak to your father."

With a grateful smile, Charlotte hugged James tightly and thanked him before dashing off to her room. Olivia watched her go, relief mixed with apprehension regarding the conversation that awaited her with James.

"She's really taken with you." James broke the silence that had settled between them.

"Yes," Olivia agreed, unable to deny the bond that was forming between her and Charlotte.

"Do not take that for granted." His gaze met hers with a seriousness that made her pause. "My greatest concern is that she builds a place in her heart for you, only for you to leave her when she needs you the most."

Olivia opened her mouth to argue, to assure him of her intentions, but he held up his hand, stopping her.

"I'm not trying to disparage your character, but it is a grave concern for anyone stepping into this role. And now that it's clear she likes you..." He let his voice trail off, leaving the implication hanging in the air.

"You have my word. I do not intend to go anywhere. I'm committed to this." Her cheeks flushed with a blush she couldn't explain, a mix of frustration and something else she couldn't quite identify.

"I'd appreciate seeing your lesson plans in advance," James continued, shifting the topic. "Perhaps we can meet while we break our fast, and you can discuss your intentions for that day."

Olivia bristled at the suggestion, feeling as though her professional abilities were being questioned. Nevertheless, she nodded, her response tight. "All right, I can agree to that."

He chuckled, a sound that grated on her nerves. "You think it wrong of me to ask? Perhaps wrong to be so involved in my daughter's upbringing?

"I shall try to earn your trust," Olivia replied carefully. The conversation had taken a turn she hadn't expected, and she found herself navigating a delicate balance between asserting her competence and acknowledging his concerns as Charlotte's father. She certainly wasn't prepared to answer his questions.

"Perhaps once you have a child, you'll understand why I'm so terribly protective of her." His voice softened slightly.

"I'm not sure I will ever be a mother or am fit to fulfil that role," Olivia murmured, the words slipping out more to herself than to him. It was a vulnerability she hadn't intended to reveal.

"You are." His conviction surprised her.

"How can you possibly say that when you barely know me?"

"Because I see it," he replied with a simple certainty that took her aback. "You will make a brilliant mother, Lady Olivia. Your child and your husband will be lucky to have you." He cleared his throat, as if realizing he had ventured into territory that was too personal. "I should retire to my study."

"Yes, of course." A whirlwind of emotions assailed her at his unexpected praise.

The two of them stood, an awkward moment hanging between them as they navigated the shift in their conversation. Finally, Olivia curtsied, a formal gesture that seemed to put a safe distance between them once again and left the room. His words echoed in her mind, leaving her with a mix of confusion and an unexpected warmth that she couldn't quite shake off.

Chapter Ten

James tossed and turned in his bed, sleep eluding him as his mind replayed the events of the evening.

The image of Olivia, a smudge of dirt on her cheek, kept surfacing in his thoughts, unbidden and unwelcome. He couldn't shake the memory of touching her face, the warmth of her skin under his fingertips, the way her eyes had widened in surprise. He reprimanded himself, trying to push away the inappropriate thoughts. She was his daughter's governess, a lady under his protection, and he had no right to think of her in such a personal manner.

As the night wore on, a sense of guilt crept in, adding to his restlessness. He'd been harsh with her about the garden, driven by a protective instinct for Charlotte and the memory of his dear duchess. But Olivia had stood her ground, challenging him in a way that few people dared. He respected her for that, even if it frustrated him.

With each passing hour, James' mind refused to quiet, the mix of attraction and guilt swirling in a tumultuous dance. He shook himself, trying to dispel the thoughts, to focus on his responsibilities and the day ahead. But the more he tried, the more elusive sleep became.

When the first light of dawn touched the sky, painting it with shades of pink and gold, James gave up on sleep. He rose from his bed, dressed quickly, and headed out for a walk in the cool morning air. The estate was peaceful at this hour, the gardens and fields shrouded in a gentle mist. He walked briskly, hoping the physical exertion would wash away the lingering thoughts of Olivia and the unsettling emotions they stirred within him.

As James rounded a bend in the garden path, he was surprised to see Olivia walking ahead of him, her head buried in a book. He quickened his pace to catch up with her, curious about what had captivated her attention so early in the morning.

"Good morning, Lady Olivia." He was suddenly and disconcertingly unsure of how to address her after their argument yesterday. "What are you reading?"

Olivia gave a start. "Good morning, Your Grace." It looked like she was as uncertain as he. She held the book for him to see. "It's 'The Long Night' by Emily Abernathy. Have you read it?"

James raised an eyebrow, surprised by her choice. "Indeed, I have. It's quite a dark and tumultuous tale. Not exactly light morning reading."

Olivia smiled, a hint of challenge in her eyes. "I find it fascinating, actually. The depth of the characters, the intensity of their emotions. It's a stark contrast to the tranquillity of the morning, but perhaps that's what makes it so compelling."

They debated the merits of the book for a few moments, James expressing his view that the characters were too driven by their passions, while Olivia argued for the beauty in their raw, unbridled emotions.

After a pause, James offered a recommendation. "If you're interested in something a bit different, you might enjoy 'Solace' by Camara Austen. It's in my library if you'd like to borrow it when you're finished with that one."

Olivia's eyes lit up at the suggestion. "Thank you, I'd like that." Her earlier animosity seemed to be forgotten in the face of their shared interest in literature.

As they neared the manor, James offered to walk Olivia back inside. "I'm surprised to see you in the gardens this early."

"It's the only time I have to read." Olivia's tone held a hint of wistfulness. "And you? Why are you up and in the gardens so early?"

James was taken aback by her directness. He hesitated for a moment before admitting, "I could not sleep." He didn't add that thoughts of her had plagued him all night. Memories of touching her face, the warmth of her skin, and her surprised eyes. He'd scolded himself for these thoughts. She was his daughter's governess, under his protection, and such personal reflections were inappropriate. And he'd been unduly harsh about the garden, driven by his protective instincts for Charlotte and memories of his late wife. Not that it was any excuse.

Once inside, Olivia took a seat at the dining table and pulled a folded piece of paper from the book. "I have prepared a lesson plan for today, as you instructed."

Discomfort twinged in his shoulders at her words. His suggestion for her to submit her lesson plans might have come across as overly controlling, and he regretted the implication. He listened as she outlined her plan for the day, and despite his initial reservations, he found himself drawn to the sound of her voice. It was calm and measured, with a warmth that he had not noticed before. He couldn't help but focus on her mouth, the way her lips moved with each word. It took some effort to concentrate on what she was saying, not just how she was saying it.

Olivia cleared her throat and smoothed the paper in front of her. She met his gaze with a direct confidence he found unusual in a young woman. "We will start today with basic arithmetic. Charlotte seems to enjoy numbers, so I'd like to build on that interest."

James nodded, indicating for her to continue.

"I have selected a few short stories that are both entertaining and educational. They have themes of friendship and kindness, which I think are important values for Charlotte to learn."

"That sounds reasonable." James was impressed by her thoughtfulness.

"Then, for something a bit more hands-on, I have planned a nature walk." She lifted her gaze to his. "It's an opportunity for Charlotte to learn about the local flora and fauna, and I will introduce her to flower pressing. I believe it's important for her to have a connection with the natural world around her."

James found himself nodding along, pleasantly surprised by the variety and creativity of Olivia's lesson plan. "It sounds like a well-rounded day. Thank you for putting so much thought into it."

Olivia smiled, a hint of relief in her expression. "I want to make sure Charlotte's education is both enjoyable and enriching."

As they finished discussing the lesson plan, Charlotte came bounding down the stairs, her energy palpable even from a distance. She greeted them with a bright smile, taking her seat at the table with infectious enthusiasm. Olivia served her breakfast, and they began to eat, the earlier tension between James and Olivia dissipating in Charlotte's presence.

During the meal, the conversation flowed easily, mostly centred around their plans for the day. Olivia subtly guided Charlotte to talk about what she hoped to learn during their nature walk, and James listened with a growing sense of pride in his daughter's curiosity. It was a pleasant change from the usual silence that had settled over their meals in recent months.

As they finished their breakfast, James glanced at the clock. He stood, excusing himself with a nod to Olivia.

"I'll leave you in Lady Olivia's capable hands, Charlotte." He smiled at his daughter, his voice warm with a newfound respect for the governess.

Charlotte beamed at him, then turned to Olivia with an excited glint in her eyes, clearly looking forward to the day's lessons. His daughter was in good hands. James walked to his study with a lightness in his step that had not been there in a while. A sense of hope that maybe, just maybe, things were starting to change for the better.

James set about his work with every intention of focusing solely on the tasks at hand, but his thoughts kept drifting back to Olivia. His chest tightened. The memory of their conversation that morning, the sound of her voice, and even the image of her sitting at the breakfast table lingered in his mind, unbidden and unwelcome.

As the morning progressed, despite every trick he knew to stay laser focused on his work, his distraction only seemed to grow. After re-reading the same parliamentary document multiple times, unable to fully concentrate on the words in front of him, he tossed it across his study.

He rubbed at his temples. He must calm down and think straight. Olivia drew emotions from him that he had not felt in years. Perhaps he could just avoid her? Or soak in a cold bath to punish himself for his wayward thoughts?

It was unlike him to be so scattered. Frustration mounting, he gathered the papers and tossed them on his desk.

During a meeting with his steward, his lack of focus became embarrassingly apparent. Mid-conversation, he realized he had completely missed a crucial point the man had raised, and he'd had to ask for the whole thing to be explained again. His steward had not complained of course, but he had noy hidden his lifted brow.

He brushed it off with a vague excuse, but internally, he recognized the truth. His thoughts of Olivia were intruding on his professional life. This was dangerous territory... she was a young lady under his care. He had to maintain the integrity of his position, and no let a momentary attraction interfere with the bourgeoning relationship between Olivia and Charlotte.

He resolved to put Olivia out of his mind, focusing solely on his work. He would maintain a professional distance and make a conscious effort to avoid any unnecessary interactions with Olivia. He'd prevent his personal feelings from clouding his judgment again.

However, his plan was short-lived as Olivia sought him out to discuss the day's events.

Her smile almost undid all his determination. She dropped into a small curtsy. "Your Grace, I wanted to talk to you about something Charlotte mentioned today."

He did not ask her to call him James again. Professional distance, he repeated to himself in a mantra in his head. Keeping his expression neutral, he nodded in response. "Go on."

"Charlotte asked if we might go into town to pick up a few books. And she needs some new gloves for our outdoor activities. I thought it might be a good opportunity for her to have a change of scenery, I will be happy to take her."

James considered the request. He knew Charlotte had been cooped up in the manor for too long, and a trip to town might be a welcome distraction. "You can go this weekend," he conceded, trying to sound nonchalant.

Olivia nodded, a small smile of appreciation on her lips. "Thank you. She will be thrilled."

So much for avoiding Olivia. What a futile thought had been. Despite his intentions, the woman was becoming an integral part of their lives, both professionally and personally. The last six years had passed in routine that was marked by the coming and going of governesses and a small celebratory meal for each of Charlotte's birthdays. Olivia's in his household would no doubt bring many more changes.

No one could deny the difference in Charlotte due to Olivia's influence. The young girl seemed more engaged, more eager to learn, and there was a light in her eyes that had been missing for some time. It was clear that Olivia's approach to teaching and her ability to connect with Charlotte on a personal level, were having a positive impact. She was not only educating his daughter but also nurturing her spirit in a way that previous governesses had failed to do.

Olivia was excelling in her role, a reality that James found both comforting and unsettling. As he observed her dedication and the remarkable progress Charlotte was making, he couldn't help but feel a surge of admiration. However, there was something more, a stirring within him that went beyond professional appreciation. Each time her image flickered through his mind, which happened far too often, he hastily shoved those disquieting thoughts aside, reminding himself of the boundaries that must govern their interactions. Still, watching Charlotte flourish under Olivia's tutelage filled him with an unexpected gratitude, mingling with a tumult of emotions that he struggled to comprehend. What was it about Olivia that unsettled him so? And could these feelings threaten the careful balance he had strived to maintain in his household?

Chapter Eleven

As the weeks passed, Olivia settled into a comfortable rhythm at Wallingford Manor. She had always expected to connect with Charlotte in a way that went beyond the usual governess relationship but teaching Charlotte had become a calling.

The child had shown remarkable improvements and seemed to thrive under her guidance. Charlotte's curiosity was insatiable, her enthusiasm for learning infectious. Olivia felt such a sense of pride in the progress they were making together that her letters home were filled with stories of their adventures in learning, the challenges they faced, and the triumphs they celebrated. It was a way to stay connected to her sisters and share a piece of her new world with them.

In the mornings, Olivia often walked in the wonderful gardens with James. Their conversations, initially centred around Charlotte and her education, gradually expanded to include discussions about books, life, and everything in between. She started to look forward to these meetings, to the easy camaraderie that had developed between them. He was becoming a friend. Of course, it was inappropriate and dangerous to feel this way about her employer, but she couldn't help herself.

The more time she spent with James, the more she saw beyond the stern exterior of the duke. He was thoughtful, intelligent, and surprisingly kind. His passion for his daughter's well-being and his dedication to his responsibilities were admirable. Olivia found herself drawn to him, not just as a father or a duke, but as a man.

Despite her growing feelings, Olivia knew she had to tread carefully. Her position at the manor, her relationship with Charlotte, and her reputation were all at stake. She resolved to keep her emotions in check, focusing on her role as a governess and companion and the difference she was making in Charlotte's life.

But as days went by, she couldn't shake the feeling that what was developing between herself and James was something she might not be able to control.

One overcast morning, Olivia stepped out for her usual walk, expecting to find James waiting for her as he often did. However, this time he was nowhere to be seen. Her shoulders dropped as an unexpected pang of disappointment hit her chest. She really had come to look forward to their morning encounters more than she cared to admit.

After finishing her solitary walk, Olivia headed inside, curious about the duke's absence. She found him in his study, surrounded by stacks of paperwork, looking more burdened than usual. "Are you well?" she asked, concern lacing her voice.

James looked up from his papers, a weary expression on his face. "The Prince Regent will be visiting the area, and it has been suggested to me that I need to throw a ball to mark the occasion."

He shivered as if the very idea gave him the chills.

Olivia laughed. "It seems the thought of a ball, little more than a matchmaking market yet lathered in pomp and pretence, is as appealing to you as it is to me."

To her surprise, James started laughing, his rich baritone even more pleasant when laughter laced his voice. "You don't like balls? I thought all women loved the chance to dress up and dance."

"I'm not all women," Olivia retorted.

"No, you are not." His laughter subsided. "I've learned as much." There was a hint of admiration in his eyes, a recognition of her uniqueness that made Olivia's heart skip a beat.

James leaned back in his chair, a curious glint in his eyes. "So, you think all balls are designed by mother hens looking for eligible marriage partners for their precious offspring?"

Olivia nodded, her expression serious. "Yes, I do. They seem to be more about matchmaking than anything else. It's all very superficial."

He studied her intently for a moment before venturing, "And what of you, Olivia? Are you promised or otherwise engaged?"

The question took Olivia by surprise, igniting a flush that tinted her cheeks. "No, no, not at all," she faltered, clearly disconcerted by the abrupt shift to a personal tone in their exchange.

"Really?" James's tone was rich with curiosity. "I would have assumed a woman of your intellect and allure would be besieged by admirers."

Olivia shifted, her discomfort palpable. "I've never much cared for that sort of attention," she confessed softly. "I've always valued a more sincere, profound connection."

James's expression softened, a glimmer of respect flashing across his features. "That is admirable," he remarked, his voice gentler. "It is indeed a rarity to encounter someone who prefers substance to spectacle."

Emboldened by their candid conversation, Olivia blurted out. "And what about you, James? Are you looking to marry again?"

The moment the words left her lips, she regretted them. It was not her place to pry into his personal life. She braced herself for his response, fearing she had overstepped her bounds. James was silent for a moment, his expression inscrutable. Then, he spoke, his voice steady but tinged with an emotion she couldn't quite identify. "No, I'm not looking for a wife," he said. "I won't put Charlotte through that. Her well-being is my priority, and I don't believe bringing a new person into our lives in that capacity would be in her best interest."

A sense of relief that he didn't seem offended by her question washed over her, followed immediately by an aching sadness for the loneliness that his decision implied. She understood his dedication to his daughter, admired it even, but he was denying himself happiness, and how would that help Charlotte in the long term?

The unexpected personal exchange left her both unsettled and strangely pleased. It seemed that James, too, preferred substance to superficiality, a revelation that only deepened her growing regard for him.

She needed to steer the conversation back to safer territory. "Who has made the request and got you in a such a pucker?"

"Just my formidable aunt."

Olivia immediately pictured Lady Beatrice and her cronies and lifted her brow.

"Not to mention the council, the Mayor and the Palace."

She had to clench her jaw to stop her mouth from dropping open. The Ducal lifestyle was way beyond what she was used to. "Then I imagine you will be holding a ball."

James grimaced. "Indeed. And I wanted you to be aware."

"Oh." Of course, he would not want his daughter's governess around for what would no doubt be a splendid affair. "Yes, I can keep to my room—"

"What?" James asked, his brow furrowing in confusion.

Olivia's cheeks warmed with embarrassment. "You will need me out of the way, of course. I quite understand."

He laughed again. "Why would you assume I would want to lock you in your room?"

"I'm the hired help, Your Grace." She couldn't understand the touch of bitterness creeping into her tone.

His brow rose even higher. "My gardener's assistant from the village is hired help. You are a guest here, as well as Charlotte's mentor and confidant. You are also Lady Olivia."

"It is still not appropriate for me to attend. Tongues will wag."

As she turned to leave, James reached out and caught her wrist, halting her departure. The touch sent a jolt through her, and she could see from his expression that he felt it too. The unexpected spark of connection left them both momentarily stunned, the tension between them suddenly charged with a new, undeniable energy.

"Do you care if they do?" James's voice trailed off, but he didn't release her wrist. The intensity in his eyes was palpable, leaving Olivia at a loss for words. Her heart hammered in her chest as the warmth of his touch seeped into her skin.

She waited, unsure of what was happening between them, but he finally spoke, his voice softer than before. "I will take your fears into consideration."

His thumb drew gentle circles on her wrist. The gesture was intimate, unexpected, and it sent a shiver down her spine.

Charlotte appeared, breaking the spell that had woven itself around them. Olivia let out a breath she had not realized she was holding, secretly grateful for the interruption and Charlotte's uncanny knack for showing up at just the right time.

James immediately released Olivia's wrist, and the moment passed as quickly as it had come.

"Did I hear you mention a ball?" She pranced into the room. "I will dance like a fairy, and everyone will clap in delight."

James sat back. "Now Charlotte you are far too young—"

"No, I'm not. I'm not too young, am I Lady Olivia?" The little minx cast a pout in Olivia's direction.

"Children don't usually attend grown up balls, Charlotte," Olivia said more brusquely than she intended.

"Anyway, I'm starving," Charlotte announced, oblivious to the tension she had just diffused.

"Let's get you something to eat." Olivia's tone was too bright. She was grateful for an excuse to escape the charged atmosphere of James' study. But as she led Charlotte away, his gaze bore into her back, a silent reminder of the connection that had just been revealed and the questions it left unanswered.

As the weeks progressed, the preparations for the ball were in full swing, transforming Wallingford Manor into a bustling hub of activity. Amidst the flurry of decorations and arrangements, Olivia found herself tasked with a new challenge: teaching Charlotte how to dance. Given the negotiations between father and daughter, it was now a crucial skill for the upcoming event, and one that Charlotte was eager to master.

She hired the same dance teacher who had been engaged for herself and her sisters. Every afternoon, the grand ballroom became their private dance studio, the polished floor reflecting their movements as they practiced step after step. Olivia was patient and encouraging, helping to guiding Charlotte through the basic steps of the English County Dance and Cotillion. They roped in as many staff as were available to make up the long lines of dancers.

Charlotte was a quick learner, her excellent memory and natural enthusiasm making up for any initial clumsiness.

As the days went by, Charlotte's confidence on the dance floor grew, her steps became polished, and pride in her young pupil swelled Olivia's chest. The upcoming ball was no longer just a social obligation for either of them. For Charlotte, it was an opportunity to show herself to the society she'd heard so much about, an opportunity for her to shine, to showcase the grace and poise she had learned. For Olivia, it was a reminder of the impact she was having on Charlotte's life, a tangible measure of the difference she was making as a governess and as a mentor.

A week or so before the ball James made an announcement that caught her off guard.

He interrupted their studies in the schoolroom. "I've organised a modiste. She arrives tomorrow to take your and Charlotte's measurements for gowns." His tone carried an air of finality that suggested it was not open for discussion.

Charlotte jumped up, clapping her hands in delight. Olivia blinked in surprise. "That is not necessary." A knot made itself known in her stomach. "I have already sent for gowns from home."

"No doubt last year's gowns." He pursed his lips. "I will not have either of you in anything but the latest fripperies and colours."

"Really, Your Grace, it's not appropriate at all."

James' gaze fixed on her, intense and unwavering. "I insist," he said, his eyes holding hers in a way that sent an unexpected shiver through her. There was something in his look that she couldn't quite decipher, a depth that was both intriguing and unsettling.

Swallowing hard, Olivia found her mouth dry, her usual composure slipping. She nodded, managing a subdued, "Thank you," even as her mind spun with a mix of emotions. As soon as James agreed to let Charlotte attend for a short while at the beginning of the ball, Olivia knew she would have to attend as well, And James had made it clear that he expected her to stay a good deal longer than Charlotte. The ball, which had seemed like a distant event, was suddenly very real and very imminent.

She returned to Charlotte's lessons, but they were both distracted, their thoughts a whirlwind, though probably for different reasons.

Olivia hated balls. Everyone knew it. But then there was James. Would he dance? Would he be different, more relaxed, during the festivities? And if he asked her to dance what would she do?

The notion was ludicrous. She chided herself, shaking her head to clear it of such foolish thoughts. And yet, she couldn't entirely dismiss the flutter of excitement that the idea sparked within her.

What might the night hold if they both forgot who they were?

Chapter Twelve

The night of the ball had finally arrived, and James found himself in his chambers, meticulously adjusting his formal attire. There was an unusual flutter in his stomach, a nervousness he couldn't quite place. He was no stranger to social events, having hosted and attended countless balls over the years, yet there was something different about tonight, a sense of anticipation that was both unfamiliar and unsettling.

As he fastened his cufflinks, James's thoughts drifted to Olivia. The image of her in a ballgown, her eyes sparkling with excitement, flashed through his mind, and his heart skipped a beat. The realization caught him off guard, and he immediately pushed it aside. It was preposterous to think that his unease had anything to do with her. She was his daughter's governess. A member of his staff, nothing more.

Despite his efforts to focus on the task at hand, James couldn't shake the feeling that the evening ahead would be unlike any other. The ballroom had been transformed, the chandeliers casting a soft glow over the elegantly dressed guests. Yet, all he could think about was Olivia's reaction to the grandeur, and whether she would be enchanted or overwhelmed.

He took a deep breath, trying to steady his nerves. He was the Duke of Ashford, the host of the evening's festivities. It was his responsibility to ensure that everything went smoothly, that his guests enjoyed themselves. He couldn't afford to be distracted, especially not by thoughts of Olivia.

As he made his way to the ballroom, James steeled himself for the night ahead. He would be the perfect host, charming and gracious, keeping his personal feelings firmly in check. Olivia was a part of his household, but tonight, she was just another guest. He would treat her with the same courtesy and respect as everyone else, nothing more. It was the only way to maintain the proper boundaries and keep his emotions at bay.

The ballroom of Ashford Manor was transformed into a breathtaking spectacle for the evening's festivities. The marble floors shone like mirrors, reflecting the soft, golden light from the crystal chandeliers that dangled majestically from the high ceilings. These chandeliers, with their intricate designs and sparkling gems, cast a warm, inviting glow that bathed the room in a magical ambiance. The walls, adorned with rich tapestries depicting scenes of historical grandeur and fine art encased in gilded frames, added an air of sophistication and timelessness to the setting.

Floral arrangements bursting with vibrant hues of roses, lilies, and peonies, were strategically placed around the room, their sweet fragrance mingling with the scent of polished wood and perfumed guests. The large windows were draped with heavy velvet curtains, framing the moonlit sky and adding to the room's opulent ambiance.

A small orchestra, consisting of violins, cellos, and a harp, was stationed at one end of the ballroom. Their music, a mix of classical compositions and lively waltzes, filled the air, inviting guests to lose themselves in the rhythm and melody. The tones of the strings, combined with the gentle clinking of champagne glasses and the soft rustle of silk gowns, created a symphony of sounds that was both exhilarating and soothing.

The guests themselves were a sight to behold. The ladies, dressed in their finest gowns, sparkled with jewels and moved with a grace that was both practised and natural. Their gowns, in shades of sapphire, emerald, and ruby, flowed elegantly as they danced, each movement accentuating their beauty and elegance. The gentlemen, equally dapper in their tailored suits and crisp white shirts, moved with confident ease, their polished shoes gliding effortlessly across the floor.

As the evening progressed, the dance floor became a whirl of colour and movement. Couples glided with a perfect blend of precision and passion, their bodies moving in harmony to the music. Laughter and conversation filled the room, creating an atmosphere of joy and celebration. It was a night that captured the essence of Ashford Manor's legacy—a celebration of beauty, elegance, and the joy of living in the moment.

As James surveyed the ballroom, his gaze searching the crowd, Charlotte was escorted to him by one of the household staff. He couldn't help but feel a twinge of disappointment that Olivia wasn't by her side. He had grown accustomed to seeing them together, and he was curious to see how Olivia would look in her gown.

Charlotte curtsied gracefully before her father, a picture of youthful elegance in her ballgown. "You look lovely, Charlotte," James commended, his heart swelling with pride at her impeccable manners. "And your curtsy is perfect."

"Thank you, Father," Charlotte replied, a hint of excitement in her voice. She was clearly thrilled to be a part of the evening's festivities.

James extended his hand to her. "May I have this dance?" he asked, a smile tugging at the corners of his mouth.

Charlotte wrinkled her nose playfully, a remnant of her usual spirited self. "I suppose," she said with mock reluctance, but her eyes sparkled with joy.

As they stepped onto the dance floor, James led his daughter in a gentle waltz, savouring the moment and the connection he shared with Charlotte. Despite his initial disappointment, he realized that this dance with his daughter was a special memory in the making, one that he would cherish for years to come.

As they glided across the dance floor, James was taken aback by how much Charlotte had improved. Her steps were sure and graceful, a far cry from the hesitant movements she had exhibited just a few weeks ago. She followed his lead with ease, her laughter ringing out as they twirled around the room. It was a delightful sight, and James couldn't help but feel a surge of gratitude towards Olivia. It was clear that her patient teaching and encouragement had played a significant role in Charlotte's newfound confidence on the dance floor.

With each step, James felt a growing sense of admiration for Olivia's dedication to his daughter's education and well-being. Charlotte's progress was a testament to Olivia's skill and commitment as a governess. As they continued to dance, James found himself more and more impressed with the positive influence Olivia had on Charlotte. It was a reminder of the invaluable role she played in their lives, and he couldn't help but feel thankful for her presence at Ashford Manor.

As the dance came to an end and James escorted Charlotte back to the edge of the dance floor, he caught sight of Olivia making her entrance into the ballroom. Time seemed to slow as he took in her appearance. She was breathtaking in her gown, the fabric accentuating her graceful figure, and her hair styled elegantly. There was a glow about her, a radiance that seemed to draw the eyes of many guests, not just his own.

James found himself unable to look away, captivated by the sight of her. It was as if he was seeing her for the first time, not just as Charlotte's governess, but as a woman in her own right. The realization took him by surprise, stirring emotions he had not anticipated. He was aware of the murmurs and glances of those around him, but his focus remained solely on Olivia as she mingled gracefully among the guests.

The intensity of his gaze did not go unnoticed. Olivia, feeling the weight of his stare, looked up and their eyes met across the crowded room. There was a moment of silent acknowledgment, a spark of something unspoken between them. James felt a jolt of electricity at the connection, a mix of admiration and something deeper, more profound. It was a feeling he couldn't quite define that both intrigued and unnerved him.

Charlotte, noticing her father's rapt attention on Olivia, leaned in and whispered, "You should ask Miss Darrow for a dance, Father."

James felt his ears turn red at the suggestion. "That would not be appropriate, Charlotte," he replied, trying to maintain a semblance of composure. The thought of dancing with Olivia, being that close to her, sent a wave of conflicting emotions through him.

"If you don't, someone else will," Charlotte warned, a mischievous glint in her eye. She had always been perceptive, and it seemed she had picked up on the unspoken tension between her father and Olivia.

As if on cue, one of James's colleagues, a distinguished gentleman known for his charm, approached Olivia and struck up a conversation. James watched as they laughed together, a knot forming in his chest. He was surprised by the intensity of his reaction, a sharp pang of jealousy coursing through him. It was a frustrating realisation, one that he couldn't quite reconcile with his role as her employer. The evening was turning out to be more complicated than he had anticipated, and he found himself at a loss for how to navigate the turbulent waters of his emotions.

As someone approached James to strike up a conversation, he barely registered their presence. His attention was entirely focused on Olivia and her dance partner, watching them with an intensity that surprised even himself. The person attempting to engage him in conversation eventually walked away, realising that James was not responding, lost in his own world.

When the music finally dimmed and the dance ended, James found himself moving towards Olivia almost instinctively. He swept her away from the crowd before she could protest. "You looked like you were enjoying yourself," he commented, trying to sound casual.

Olivia, caught off guard by his sudden appearance, replied, "As women, our true thoughts and feelings are often hidden underneath the mask of painted faces and braided hair." Her words held a depth that made James pause, considering the layers of meaning behind them.

Without fully understanding why, he found himself pulling her away from the ballroom, out into the cool night air of the gardens. "You should be careful with my colleagues," he warned her, his tone more serious now. "Some of them are not as honourable as they seem."

Olivia turned to him, her expression one of mild annoyance. "I'm not interested in your colleagues, James," she said firmly. "I can handle myself."

Their conversation quickly escalated into an argument, their voices rising in the quiet of the garden. "You don't understand the games they play," James insisted, his concern for her safety mixing with his own confused feelings.

"And you don't understand that I'm not some delicate flower that needs protecting," Olivia shot back, her frustration evident. "I'm here for Charlotte, not to find a husband among your friends."

The tension between them was palpable, their argument fuelled by emotions neither of them fully understood. As they stood there, facing each other in the moonlit garden, it was clear that their relationship had reached a turning point, one that could change everything.

"I'm not trying to protect you," James said, his voice firm. "I'm just telling you the truth so you will be better informed."

Olivia's eyes flashed with defiance. "I'm not interested in being informed either way," she retorted, her stance unwavering.

He couldn't help but let out a frustrated sigh. "You are so stubborn," he muttered, the words slipping out before he could stop them.

Her expression turned cold at the accusation. "I am offended that you would call me that," she said, her voice sharp with indignation.

In that heated moment, something inside James snapped. Before he fully realised what he was doing, he closed the distance between them and kissed her. It was a kiss born of frustration, confusion, and an undeniable attraction that had been simmering beneath the surface for far too long.

James pulled away, a mixture of shock and regret washing over him. He opened his mouth to apologize, to try and salvage the situation, but before he could utter a word, Olivia reached up and pulled him back towards her. Her lips met his in a kiss that was both unexpected and electrifying.

This time, James did not resist. He let himself get lost in the moment, in the feel of her lips against his, the warmth of her body close to his. All thoughts of propriety and the reasons why this was a bad idea faded away. In that moment, there was only Olivia and the undeniable connection that had drawn them together despite their best efforts to keep it at bay.

Chapter Thirteen

The kiss left Olivia feeling exhilarated, a rush of emotions swirling inside her that she had never experienced before. It was as if the world had tilted on its axis, and nothing would ever be the same again. When James finally pulled away, she saw the apology forming on his lips, but she shook her head, silencing him. She did not want to hear it, nor did she want to tarnish the intensity of the moment they had just shared.

He gave her a long, assessing look, his eyes tracing the contours of her face. "Your hair is askew," he said, a hint of concern in his voice. "You need to repair it, or people will be suspicious."

The practicality of his words brought Olivia back to reality, a reminder of the consequences their actions could have.

He offered to walk her to her bedroom, a gesture that should have comforted her, but instead left her feeling dejected.

It was silly to feel this way, she told herself. She tried to shake off the sense of disappointment, to not let herself get caught up in the moment. But as they walked back to the manor, the silence between them heavy with unspoken words, Olivia couldn't help but feel a pang of regret. The kiss, as thrilling as it had been, had opened a door that she was not sure they could close again.

Back in her room, Olivia stared at her reflection in the mirror, trying to smooth her hair back into place. Her mind replayed the kiss over and over, each detail etched into her memory with startling clarity. She knew things had changed between her and James, and they had crossed a line that could not be ignored. The question now was what they would do about it? How they would navigate the tangled web of emotions and responsibilities that lay before them?

After repairing her hair, Olivia stepped out of her room only to find James waiting for her in the hallway. His expression was serious, and he wasted no time in addressing the situation. "I promise that will never happen again," he said, his tone firm. "It was unbecoming of me."

Olivia bristled at his words, feeling a mix of anger and hurt. "I did not ask for you to kiss me," she retorted, her voice sharp. "You kissed me all on your own."

James seemed taken aback by her defensiveness. "I do not understand why you are being so defensive," he said, confusion evident in his voice.

"And I do not understand how you don't understand," Olivia shot back, her frustration growing. She could not believe he was trying to place the blame on her.

Before either of them knew what was happening, they were drawn together once again, their lips meeting in a kiss that was filled with all the tension and unresolved emotions between them. It was as if they were both unable to resist the pull, the undeniable attraction that had sparked the moment their lips had first touched.

"You are so...blasted...stubborn," he murmured against her mouth.

"Perhaps," she said. "But I..."

She let her voice trail off, suddenly shy.

Her body was a cast of emotions — elation, desirous, needy, scared, concerned. She did not know what to feel first and what to put away.

His eyes darkened, as if he could read her mind.

"Miss Darrow," he murmured.

"Olivia," she said automatically.

"Are you sure?"

She nodded once.

"I'm not entirely certain —"

"Do you dare tell me how you think I am supposed to feel?" she asked, much bolder than she truly felt.

Something in James snapped. He grabbed her arms and dragged her back into her room, kicking the door shut behind them before claiming her lips with his.

Their kiss deepened, a whirlwind of emotions swirling between them as they surrendered to the intoxicating pull of desire. For Olivia, it was a dizzying revelation, a tumultuous blend of longing and uncertainty that consumed her every thought. In that moment, there were no apologies or regrets, only the raw intensity of their connection igniting like wildfire.

As the outside world faded into insignificance, they clung to each other in a desperate embrace, their hearts beating as one in the echoing silence of the room. James' touch was electric against her skin, sending shivers down her spine and awakening a hunger that she never knew existed. In his arms, Olivia felt both vulnerable and empowered, a paradox of emotions that left her breathless and yearning for more.

When they finally broke apart, gasping for air with flushed cheeks and entwined fingers, James gazed at her with an intensity that took her breath away. There was a vulnerability in his eyes that mirrored her own.

"Help me?" she asked, turning to give him her back.

James' eyes darkened, and he began to slowly unfasten the bodice of the gown she wore.

Their hearts beat in synchrony as they stood there in that intimate moment, the air thick with unspoken desires and uncharted territories. Olivia's pulse quickened at the feel of James' hands on her skin, his touch setting her alight with a fire that threatened to consume them both. As he continued to undress her with a tenderness that belied the passion simmering between them, Olivia felt a rush of emotions flood her senses, overwhelming her with a heady mix of anticipation and uncertainty.

She turned to face him, her eyes locking with his in a silent exchange of unspoken promises. In that moment, nothing else mattered but the connection they shared, the magnetic pull drawing them closer with each passing heartbeat.

"I...I don't know what to do," she admitted.

His eyes widened, and she instantly saw him hesitate. "Perhaps I should —"

"I want you to teach me," she said. And then, "Please."

James studied her intently, his gaze searching hers for any sign of hesitation. Seeing none, he nodded slowly and took her hand, leading her to the small sitting area by the window. They sat in silence for a moment, the only sound filling the room the soft rustle of fabric and the quiet hum of their mingled breaths.

"Olivia," James began, his voice low and gentle. "Desire is a powerful force, but it must be tempered with trust and respect. Are you sure you want this?"

Her heart pounded in her chest as she met his gaze without flinching. "Yes," she whispered, her voice barely audible.

With a nod, James leaned in to capture her lips in a tender kiss, a promise of what was to come. His hands moved with practised precision, undressing her slowly and reverently, each touch igniting a fire within her that threatened to consume her whole until she was completely bare before him.

As the last piece of fabric fell to the floor, Olivia stood before James in all her vulnerability, her heart pounding with a mixture of fear and anticipation. His gaze roamed over her, his eyes dark with desire and something more profound that she couldn't quite decipher. In that moment, there was a silent understanding between them, a mutual recognition of the weight of their actions and the unspoken promises they were making.

Without a word, James took her hand and led her to the bed, his touch gentle yet firm as he guided her to lie down. Olivia's breath caught in her throat as he hovered over her, his eyes locked on hers with a tenderness that made her heart ache. And then, slowly, he began to explore her with a reverence that left her trembling with need.

Every touch, every caress felt like a revelation, as if James was unravelling layers of her soul that she had kept hidden even from herself. In his arms, she felt exposed yet safe, protected, cherished. The sensations were overwhelming, the intensity building steadily until her entire being seemed to shimmer with desire.

James trailed featherlight kisses along her neck and down her chest, his hands teasing and caressing every inch of her skin. She arched into his touch, a silent plea for more, and he responded with a deep groan that reverberated through her body.

"Are you sure?" he asked again, his voice hoarse with passion.

She nodded, her eyes never leaving his. "Yes," she whispered, the word barely audible.

With a gentle smile, James continued his exploration, his lips tracing a path down her stomach and lower still. Olivia's breath hitched in her throat as she felt his mouth on her, the sensation sending waves of pleasure coursing through her veins. Her fingers tightened in his hair, urging him closer, wanting more.

And then he touched her there, his fingers exploring the most intimate part of her body, sending shockwaves of pleasure radiating from her core. Olivia moaned softly, her hips bucking against his touch, lost in the sheer intensity of the sensation.

James continued his exploration, his tongue replacing his fingers, his lips and tongue working their magic on her most sensitive spot. She writhed beneath him, her body on fire with a need she had never known before. Her breath came in ragged gasps, her heart pounding in her ears as she surrendered to the exquisite pleasure he was giving her.

As the tension built, Olivia felt herself teetering on the edge of ecstasy, every muscle in her body taut with anticipation. She cried out his name, her body arching off the bed as she shattered into a million pieces, her release crashing over her like a tidal wave.

When she finally came back to herself, she found herself cradled in James's arms, his heart beating steadily against her chest. He was staring down at her, his eyes filled with a mix of tenderness and satisfaction.

"Are you okay?" he asked softly, his fingers gently tracing the outline of her features.

Olivia smiled up at him, feeling a warmth spread through her that had nothing to do with the pleasure she'd just experienced. Instead, it was a sense of contentment and happiness that she'd never known before.

"I'm more than okay," she replied, feeling a stirring in her heart that she did not quite understand.

James moved back up before pulling her into another passionate kiss. The fact that she could taste herself was more erotic than she realised, but it did not deter her from wanting more from him.

As their lips parted, Olivia found herself lost in a whirlpool of emotions. She was scared, nervous, and unsure of what to expect. But at the same time, she felt exhilarated, like she was finally living the life she had always dreamed of.

James looked into her eyes. "Are you ready?" he whispered, his breath warm against her skin.

Olivia nodded, her heart racing with excitement and fear. She was ready, even more than she expected. In truth, she never thought she would be privy to this experience, but maybe she didn't have to follow the rules in order to get what she wanted.

Maybe, with James, she could truly be herself.

Chapter Fourteen

James couldn't keep his eyes off Olivia. He still tasted her on his tongue, and the way her body responded was more than he could have hoped for, more than he expected. Carefully, he positioned himself over her.

"This will hurt," he murmured. "We can stop at any time."

Olivia nodded, her eyes locked with his, filled with trust and desire. She reached up and caressed his cheek softly, a silent reassurance that she was ready.

With a deep breath, James leaned in and pressed his lips to hers, before slowly pushing past her folds.

Olivia gasped, sinking her nails into his shoulders. He stilled, letting her adjust, but he had yet to fully sheath himself in her warmth.

"Are you all right?" he whispered, his heart pounding in his chest as he waited for her response. Olivia nodded, her eyes fluttering closed for a moment before opening them again to gaze into his. She let out a shaky breath, managing a small smile.

"I am fine," she assured him. "It's just... well, I'm not sure what I expected."

He couldn't help but chuckle softly, feeling a sense of pride at her honesty. Gently, he began to push even further until he was completely wrapped in her warmth.

He moaned, closing his eyes. Everything screamed in him to move but he simply could noot.

Not until he knew she was okay.

She looked up at him, her eyes filled with gratitude and desire. She lifted a hand and cupped his cheek.

"I'm fine," she repeated, her voice steadier this time. "It's just… different than I expected. But in a good way."

James nodded, eyes on her face, just to ensure the truth of her words. Taking a deep breath, he slowly began to move, his hips rocking gently against hers. Olivia moaned softly, her nails digging into his back as she adjusted to his rhythm. He continued at a slow pace, allowing her body to familiarise with him and accommodate him inside her.

As the minutes passed, James grew bolder with each thrust, his rhythm increasing in intensity. Olivia's moans became more frequent, her nails digging deeper into his skin as she arched her back to meet his every move. He could feel her body responding to him, becoming more receptive with each passing moment.

They moved in perfect harmony, the heat between them intensifying with each passing second. Olivia's eyes locked with his, her expression now a mix of passion and trust. He felt her fingers grip his hips, pulling him closer, urging him on.

With a low growl, he surrendered to the craving that had been building within him from the moment he first saw Olivia. His movements became more frenzied, their bodies slamming together with a fiery intensity.

"James!" she cried out. "Oh, James, please!" Her voice was filled with raw pleasure as she reached the pinnacle of her desire.

He felt her body tremble beneath him, her nails digging into his skin as the wave of pleasure washed over her. Her cries filled the room, mingling with his own moans of satisfaction. As they moved together, their bodies slick with sweat, he knew that this moment was something they would never forget.

"Olivia," he said, locking eyes with her. "Fuck, Olivia."

His own climax crept up on him, but he didn't have a chance to prepare. His pistoned in and out of her, filling her warmth with his seed as pleasure washed across his body.

Finally, he collapsed on top of her, breathing heavily and trying to catch his breath. She wrapped her arms around him, pulling him close, and they lay there for what felt like hours, basking in the afterglow of their passion.

He knew he would never forget this night, this moment. He had finally claimed her, and he knew that she was his. He was filled with a sense of satisfaction and contentment that he had never experienced before.

As James lay on the bed, staring up at the ceiling with Olivia beside him, a wave of guilt began to wash over him. He felt as though he had betrayed his late wife, the memory of their love and the promises he had made to her. It was as if he had dishonoured her memory with his actions, allowing himself to be swept away by a moment of passion with someone else.

He also felt he had betrayed Charlotte's trust. He was her father, her protector, and he had always vowed to set a good example for her. But here he was, getting lost in a moment of weakness, showing a side of himself that he never wanted his daughter to see. He could not help but wonder what Charlotte would think of him if she knew, and the thought made his heart heavy with shame.

And then there was Olivia herself. He felt guilty for having been so reckless with her, for letting their emotions get the better of them. He had always prided himself on being a man of control and honour, but in that moment, he had let all of that slip away. He had put Olivia in a difficult position, one that could potentially compromise her reputation and her position in his household.

The weight of his actions pressed down on him, and James could not shake the feeling that he had made a grave mistake. He had allowed a moment of passion to cloud his judgment, which could lead him down a path that could have serious consequences for everyone involved. He knew he needed to somehow find a way to repair the damage he had done. He couldn't help but feel a sense of dread that things might never be the same again.

"I should get back to the ball," James murmured, sitting up. He could not bring himself to look at Olivia, feeling like a coward for not facing her. He knew she deserved so much better than him, but he was at a loss for what to do. After years of burying his feelings, the intensity of what he felt now was almost painful.

"That's it, then?" Olivia asked, sitting up as well. "You are just going to leave?"

James turned back to look at her, her question hanging in the air between them. "What would you like from me?" he asked, his voice a mix of frustration and vulnerability. He was torn between his sense of duty and the undeniable connection he felt with Olivia, unsure of how to navigate the tumult of emotions he was experiencing.

James took a deep breath, trying to steady himself. "Olivia, I... I don't know what to say. This should not have happened."

Olivia's eyes flashed with a mix of emotions. "But it did happen, James. You can't just pretend it did not."

He ran a hand through his hair, feeling the weight of the situation. "I know, and I am sorry. I have put you in an impossible position."

She shook her head, a bitter laugh escaping her lips. "Sorry? Is that all you have to say? You kiss me, you bring me here, and all you can say is sorry?"

James flinched at the harshness in her voice. "I wish I could offer you more, but I... I have responsibilities. I have Charlotte to think about."

Olivia stood up, her eyes glistening with unshed tears. "And what about what I think? What about what I feel? Do those not matter to you at all?"

He stood as well, the distance between them feeling like a chasm. "Of course, they matter. But I can't just act on my feelings without considering the consequences."

She took a step back, wrapping her arms around herself. "So, what now? We just go back to pretending none of this ever happened?"

James sighed, feeling a knot in his stomach. "I don't know, Olivia. I truly don't know."

The tension in the room was palpable, a stark contrast to the passion they had shared just moments ago. Both knew that nothing would be the same after tonight, but neither had the answers to the questions that now hung between them.

James nodded, his chest clenching at her request. He approached her and carefully laced up her dress, his fingers brushing against her skin. The simple act felt charged with the weight of everything that had transpired between them.

"Olivia," he said softly, unable to stop himself from saying her name one more time.

She turned to face him, her expression unreadable. "It would probably be best if you refrain from speaking my given name," she said, her voice steady but tinged with a hint of sadness.

James felt a pang of regret as he stepped back, acknowledging the distance that had formed between them. He had wanted to protect her, to keep their relationship professional, but in one impulsive moment, he had changed everything. Now, he was left with the consequences and the knowledge that he had hurt someone he had come to care for deeply.

As Olivia left the room, James was left alone with his thoughts, grappling with the realisation that their relationship could never be the same. He had crossed a line, and now he had to face the reality of what that meant for both of them.

The ball carried on, laughter and music filling the grand ballroom, but James's heart wasn't in it. He moved through the crowd, exchanging pleasantries and playing the role of the gracious host, but his thoughts were elsewhere. He caught glimpses of Olivia throughout the evening, her laughter mingling with that of the other guests, her smile lighting up the room. He felt a surge of protectiveness when he saw her speaking with a male colleague of his, but he pushed it aside, reminding himself that she was free to converse with whomever she pleased.

As the night wore on, the hour grew late, and James knew it was time to bid Charlotte goodnight. He found her amidst a group of young guests, her cheeks flushed with excitement from the evening's festivities.

With a fatherly smile, he escorted her to her room, tucking her into bed with a soft kiss on her forehead.

"Goodnight, my dear," he whispered, feeling a pang of guilt for the turmoil that lay just beneath the surface of the evening's glamour.

Once Charlotte was settled, James made his way back to the ballroom to make his final rounds as host.

His heart wasn't in it. The greetings and praise felt hollow, a stark contrast to the emptiness he felt after his encounter with Olivia. The ball might have been a success in the eyes of his guests, but for James, it was a night he could not wait to forget.

James lingered in the quiet aftermath, the echoes of the day's events slowly fading into a profound silence that enveloped the house. It was a stark contrast to the earlier hustle and bustle, the lively conversations and laughter that had filled the space. As he made his way to his room, the emptiness seemed to press in on him, a tangible reminder of the absence he felt so acutely. Olivia's presence, or rather the lack thereof, weighed heavily on his mind. The realisation that he missed her caught him off guard. Their time together had been brief, just a single encounter, yet it had left an indelible mark on him. The depth of his longing puzzled him, stirring a mix of emotions he struggled to comprehend.

In the solitude of his room, James found himself grappling with the possibility that he might have jeopardized not only his own chance at happiness but his daughter's as well. His actions could have repercussions for them both, a burden he hadn't fully anticipated. The connection he'd felt with Olivia was unexpected, a serendipitous encounter that had blossomed into something more profound than he had dared to hope for. Yet, now, he was left to wonder if a single moment of vulnerability might have cost them both dearly.

The silence of the house seemed to amplify his fears, each tick of the clock a reminder of time slipping away, time that he could have spent forging a bond with Olivia. The hope that he had not irrevocably damaged their budding relationship was a fragile thread to cling to, yet it was all he had. As he lay in the quiet darkness, James could not shake the feeling of emptiness that Olivia's absence had left. The prospect of facing tomorrow without the possibility of seeing her again was a bleak one, leaving him to confront the consequences of his actions and the uncertain path that lay ahead.

Chapter Fifteen

Olivia woke up the morning after the ball, her mind immediately flooding with memories of the night before.

How could she let this happen? What on earth had she been thinking?

Her heart stuttered at the thought of James, of their stolen moments together, but she quickly calmed herself. She would not give in to her feelings. She had come to Wallingford Manor to escape all expectation of marriage and motherhood, and she would not let one moment of weakness derail her.

Not that James had offered marriage. Not even a place as his mistress. He'd shown her nothing but his own regrets, the cad. A wave of dizziness washed over her. She felt naked and exposed for the world's amusement. Olivia blinked back unshed tears. She had a purpose here, and now, damn good reasons to maintain distance from him.

With a deep breath, she rang for Jane and asked for a practical outfit devoid of any frills. She needed to remind herself of her purpose here, of the distance she needed to maintain. Jane must have known about her shameful behaviour, but she hadn't said a word beyond those required for politeness. Did everyone downstairs know?

She let out a pained groan, gave herself a pep talk and grabbed a book for her morning walk.

Thank goodness James wasn't waiting for her, as had become their routine. She should have been relieved, but instead she couldn't ignore the ache in her heart, the sense of loss that his absence brought.

Determined not to let it affect her, Olivia lifted her chin and set off on her walk alone. The crisp morning air was refreshing, and she focused on the beauty of the surrounding countryside, on the peace and solitude that it offered. It was a stark contrast to the turmoil in her heart, but she welcomed the distraction, grateful for the chance to clear her mind and steel herself for the day ahead.

On her return to the house, Charlotte was already at the breakfast table, animatedly chattering about the ball to a servant. James was nowhere to be seen.

"Where is the duke, Charlotte?" Olivia tried to keep her voice casual.

"He had to leave early for political meetings." Charlotte briefly diverted her attention from recounting the previous night's events.

A wave of fury swept in, hot and unyielding. Anger at herself for letting her emotions get the better of her, anger at James for leaving her in a state of confusion. She took a seat at the table, determined to keep her emotions in check.

"What are we going to do today?" Charlotte asked, her eyes bright with curiosity.

"We agreed upon a rest day to allow us to recover after the ball."

Charlotte pulled a face. "I don't want to rest."

It probably would be a good idea to distract herself with her normal routine. "We could read together. And perhaps we can check on the garden later."

Charlotte's face lit up at the mention of the garden. "Oh, I'd love that!"

Olivia forced a smile, grateful for the distraction Charlotte provided. She would focus on her duties, on Charlotte's education and well-being, and push aside the turmoil of her own emotions. It was the only way she knew how to cope with the confusion that James had brought into her life.

They read together in the morning, exploring stories that sparked Charlotte's imagination and prompted thoughtful discussions. Olivia found solace in the routine, in the simplicity of their lessons, and in Charlotte's eager curiosity.

In the afternoon, they ventured out to the garden and beyond, where Olivia taught Charlotte about the different plants and flowers, and how each played a part in the ecosystem. It was a peaceful, grounding activity, providing Olivia genuine enjoyment. The garden, with its vibrant colours and fragrant scents, provided a serene backdrop that helped Olivia push her feelings aside, if only for a while.

As the day drew to a close, Olivia ensured Charlotte was tucked into bed, listening as the young girl recounted her favourite parts of the day with a sleepy smile. Once Charlotte was asleep, Olivia retreated to the drawing room, seeking the comfort of a good book. The quiet of the room, with its soft lighting and gentle crackle of a well stoked fire, was a balm to her unsettled spirit. She lost herself in the pages, letting the words carry her away from the confusion that lingered just beneath the surface.

It was extremely late before James returned home. Olivia heard his footsteps in the hallway, but he didn't enter the drawing room and she did not look up from her book.

Olivia wasn't ready to face him, to confront the emotions his presence inevitably stirred within her. She could push her feelings aside during the day, focus on her responsibilities and Charlotte's needs, but in the quiet of the night, with James so close yet so far, it was a much more difficult task. She remained in the drawing room, reading long into the night, seeking solace in the escape that only books could provide.

The next few days followed a similar pattern. Each morning, Olivia immersed herself in her lessons with Charlotte. She found peace in the routine, in the predictability of their daily schedule. Charlotte's enthusiasm and curiosity were a constant source of joy.

But as the days passed, frustration built within her. The unresolved tension between her and James lingered like a shadow casting a pall over her otherwise content existence at Wallingford Manor. She was constantly on edge, her emotions fluctuating between anger and longing. The brief encounters she had with James were polite but distant. She felt as though she were treading lightly, careful not to provoke any further rush of emotion.

Olivia tried to push her feelings aside and focus on her responsibilities and the positive aspects of her life at the manor. But the more she tried to ignore the situation, the more frustrated she became. She was caught in limbo, unsure of how to move forward, and the uncertainty of it all was starting to wear on her.

On the third night after putting Charlotte to bed, Olivia decided she couldn't stand the tension any longer. She marched to James's study, not bothering to knock, and walked in. "This must stop.

"I beg your pardon?" He glanced up from his papers, clearly surprised by her sudden entrance.

She stood her ground, a surge of adrenalin giving her courage. "You need to start acting like an adult. We can't keep dancing around each other. Charlotte has already asked me what is wrong between us. We both need to get over this tension and return to the way things were."

There was no way she could just forget. But she was willing to put it behind her for Charlotte's sake. To her surprise, James denied he was acting differently at all.

"Are you serious?" She narrowed her eyes at him.

"Quite."

The calmness in his tone sharpened her anger. She shook her head in disbelief. "You're a coward. At least I admit that we… that something happened between us instead of pretending it didn't. For Charlotte's sake I am willing to move on. I thought you would want the same. But if this is how you're going to treat me…" She let her voice trail off, her frustration evident.

"What? What are you threatening?"

"How dare you. I am not threatening anything."

He stood, his tone suddenly sharp. "You would leave us? Leave Charlotte?"

"Of course not. I will not abandon Charlotte. But you are leaving me in a very difficult place." Olivia marched from the room with her dignity intact. She had said her piece, and now it was up to him to decide how he would move forward.

Back in her room, Olivia began the familiar routine of preparing for bed, her movements automatic, her conversation with Jane stilted, as she tried to push away the events of the evening.

It was only when she was finally alone, the door to her room locked, that the facade crumbled. The tears she had been holding back spilled over, and she slumped onto her bed, allowing herself to cry for the first time since she arrived at the Manor.

She had left her family and the life she knew to escape the confines of societal expectations and find a sense of freedom and purpose. And yet, after only a few weeks, she found herself irrevocably in love with The Duke of Wallingford, a man who was as bound by duty and convention as anyone she had ever known. It was a cruel irony, and the realisation hit her with the force of a physical blow.

Olivia mourned not just for the unrequited love she felt, but for the loss of the simplicity she had once believed she could find. She had wanted to escape the complexities of love and expectation, but they had found her anyway, in the most unexpected places. She was in love with a man who would never love her back, and the weight of that truth was almost too much to bear.

A gentle knock on the door interrupted her weeping. Olivia scrubbed at her wet cheeks. Was it James? No, he had made his choice and would not back down. Her heart skipped a beat as she got out of bed anyway and she almost tripped on her way to the door. She took a deep breath to settle herself, but it was Charlotte standing there, her eyes filled with concern.

"I heard you crying." Charlotte said, her voice soft. "Is something amiss?"

Olivia was taken aback. How could she respond? She could not possibly explain the true reason for her tears to Charlotte. Before she could find words, Charlotte spoke. "Do you miss your mommy?"

The question caught Olivia off guard, but she found herself nodding. "I do," she admitted, her voice barely a whisper. "Very much."

"Me too," Charlotte said, a hint of sadness in her voice.

Charlotte crawled into bed with Olivia, seeking comfort in her presence. Olivia wrapped her arms around the young girl, grateful for the unexpected solace they found in each other's company. As they lay there, the weight of their shared loneliness and longing seemed to lighten, and eventually, they both drifted off to sleep, finding a sense of peace in the quiet companionship of the night.

Chapter Sixteen

In the weeks that followed their confrontation, James kept his distance from Olivia, her fiery words still echoing in his mind. Conflicting emotions tumbled in his mind, guilt sitting as heavy as a stone in his chest. Yet he couldn't ignore the growing attraction he felt towards her.

Despite his efforts to stay away, James found time to secretly watch Olivia whenever she was with Charlotte. The way she interacted with his daughter, the genuine care and affection she showed, warmed his heart. He admired her, and with each passing day, he found himself wanting her more.

It was a feeling he had to suppress beneath a facade of indifference.

Olivia was right—he was a coward. But how could he risk further complicating their relationship? He could not allow his personal feelings to interfere with the well-being of his daughter or the harmony of his household. It was a sacrifice he had to make, no matter how much it pained him.

He watched Olivia and Charlotte laughing together in the garden one afternoon and ached with the longing to join them. Damn it, he wanted to share in those moments of joy. It was a desire he had to keep buried. There was no way he could be close to Olivia and not show his feelings for her.

Debbit disturbed his musing with a quiet cough. "Lord Harding is here, Your Grace. Shall I let him know you are receiving visitors?"

James was not in the mood, but having known Harding since Eton, he hoped his old friend might provide a much-needed distraction. "Send him to my study, Debbit."

Harding waltzed into the room and settled himself on the brocade settee. After exchanging a few pleasantries, James offered him a glass of brandy, which Harding half-guzzled in one gulp.

James sipped from his own glass. "What brings you out this way."

"Your governess is quite a catch." Harding gave him a sly smile. "She's Weston's sister-in-law, isn't she? I think she might make an excellent wife."

A surge of protectiveness filled James at the mention of Olivia. "Not appropriate, Harding. She's here as a companion and mentor for Charlotte, not to entertain suitors."

Harding was unperturbed by James's rejection. "Oh, come now, James. She's Lady Olivia Darrow, Her father was a peer, her demeanour impeccable. A woman of her calibre shouldn't be wasted on governess duties alone. I believe I shall call on her within the week, regardless of how you feel about it."

The casualness with which Harding spoke about Olivia ignited a spark of anger in James. "I would advise against that, Harding." His voice was tight with barely contained irritation. "Olivia is a valued member of my household, and I won't have her disturbed by unwelcome advances."

"Unwelcome, eh?" Harding shrugged, a smirk playing on his lips. "We'll see, James. We'll see."

He shifted the conversation to political matters before taking his leave. It was as if he'd just dropped by to needle James. His stomach sank to new lows. He had to find a way to protect her, even if it meant further complicating the already delicate situation between them.

James pressed his hands to his face, rifling his fingertips through his hair. He didn't have the right to shield Olivia from the attentions of others. She was her own person, free to make her own choices, and yet the thought of her with anyone else, especially someone like Harding, infuriated him. He stared at his papers without reading them.

It was a possessiveness he had no claim to, a feeling that contradicted the distance he had forced between them. His mind churned with conflicting emotions, the image of Olivia in the ballroom, laughing at something Harding said haunted him.

Harding had always been something of a libertine, known for his charm and flirtatious nature. He wasn't at all the right person for his quiet, studious Olivia. He would curtail her spirit as much as any governess did to his precious daughter. It was a bitter pill to swallow, the knowledge that he wanted to protect her, to be the one she turned to, even though he had pushed her away.

He poured himself another brandy. He would find a way to keep Olivia safe from Harding's advances without overstepping the bounds of professionalism.

Suddenly, his door burst open. He was about to yell at the culprit when Charlotte rushed to him, her face streaked with tears. "It's Olivia!" she sobbed, clinging to him. "She's sick."

The news hit James like a physical blow. Charlotte would not be so upset at a simple illness. Concern for Olivia surged through him, mingling with a sense of dread. He had been so caught up in his own turmoil that he hadn't considered her happiness. Now, faced with her illness, all his reservations fell away, replaced by a singular focus on her well-being. He had to see her to find out what was wrong and ensure she received the care she needed.

Charlotte's nanny was in the hallway waiting for Charlotte to return. But Charlotte wouldn't leave his side.

"Tell me," James demanded. "What is wrong with Lady Olivia? The urgency in his tone was unmistakable, a reflection of the worry gnawing at him.

The woman hesitated, taken aback by his intensity. Sensing her reluctance, James snapped again, "Tell me!"

Charlotte pulled away from him. With a quivering voice, she provided the details that James was desperate to hear. "She keeps vomiting. Even a glass of lemonade upsets her. She can't keep anything down." Charlotte's eyes brimmed with fresh tears.

Olivia's illness sounded serious. He shouted for Debbit. "Send for the physician immediately."

Debbit turned to carry out the order. With a sense of urgency propelling him forward, James strode to Olivia's room. He knocked softly before entering, not wanting to startle her if she was resting. The sight that greeted him tugged at his heartstrings. Olivia lay in bed, her usually vibrant face pale and drawn, a sheen of sweat on her forehead. She looked up at him with weary eyes, a shadow of her usual self.

He approached her bedside. "How are you feeling?"

She attempted a weak smile but it didn't reach her eyes. "I've been better," she admitted, her voice barely above a whisper.

Seeing her so vulnerable, so unlike the strong, spirited woman he had come to know, filled James with an overwhelming desire to help her. But apart from getting the physician, he felt helpless. "Is there anything I can do for you?"

Olivia shook her head slightly. "I Just need rest, I think. Thank you for checking on me, James."

The use of his first name rather than "Your Grace" caught him off guard, but he nodded, lingering for a moment longer, wishing there was more he could do to ease her discomfort. He could not bear the thought of her suffering.

He sat at the chair beside her bed and tried to form the words to apologise for his behaviour over the past month. The distance he had put between them, the unresolved tension—it all seemed trivial now in the face of her illness. He wanted to make amends, to start afresh and support her through her recovery.

But before he could voice his thoughts, Olivia spoke up. "You should leave," she said, a hint of concern in her voice. "And Charlotte should not be allowed to visit. I don't want either of you to catch this." Her selflessness, even in her weakened state, made his heart clench, making James admire her more.

He hesitated, torn between his desire to stay and care for her and the need to respect her wishes. But logic won out. It would not help Olivia if he and Charlotte sickened.

With a heavy heart, James nodded and quietly left the room, vowing to himself that he would do everything in his power to ensure Olivia received the best care possible.

When James stepped out of Olivia's room, he found Charlotte waiting in the hallway, her small face etched with worry. He bent forward and offered a reassuring smile, trying to infuse his words with confidence he didn't fully feel.

"Let's get you into bed."

"I'm not sleepy, Father." Charlotte narrowed her gaze at him.

"I know you are too old for an afternoon nap, but no one is too old for a short rest after a disturbing shock."

Her lip quivered, but she didn't resist when he took her hand and led her back to her own room.

He tucked her into bed with a gentle touch. Remembering the routine that Olivia had established, he picked up the book they had been sharing and began to read a chapter aloud. His voice filled the room, weaving the story into the quiet afternoon. Charlotte's mind was elsewhere, her thoughts no doubt lingering on Olivia, but at least she settled against the pillows and eventually closed her eyes.

When the chapter ended, James closed the book, hoping his daughter would drift off to sleep. But she reached out, grabbing his hand. "Don't go, please," she whispered, her eyes pleading.

James's heart ached for her. He couldn't find it in himself to deny her request.

He continued the story in quiet tones, his presence a silent promise of safety and comfort, until Charlotte's grip relaxed as she finally succumbed to sleep.

Instead of returning to his study, James wandered aimlessly through the manor. His feet led him to a familiar place: Elizabeth's rose garden. The late afternoon sun cast a soft glow over the flowers, creating a serene and almost ethereal atmosphere. He walked the spiral path among the blooms, each step heavy with the weight of his thoughts.

Reaching the centre of the garden, surrounded by the beauty his wife had once tended with such care, he felt a sudden urge to pray. He was not a man who often turned to prayer, but in that moment, it felt like the only thing he could do. Dropping to his knees, he closed his eyes and let the words spill from his heart.

He prayed for Olivia's health, for Charlotte's future, and for the strength to support them both through whatever challenges lay ahead.

He remained kneeling in silence for several moments. In this garden, Elizabeth's presence was almost palpable. He had not expected to ever desire another woman, but now that he did, the tumult in his heart and mind was an agony he had not foretold.

As he knelt there, surrounded by the fragrant roses, James glanced skyward, feeling a sense of connection to his late wife. He took a deep breath and began to whisper his concerns, his words a quiet plea to Elizabeth.

"Elizabeth," he began softly, "I never imagined I would find myself in this position, torn between duty and my heart. Olivia is so different from you, yet she has a strength and kindness that remind me of you every day. I fear for her, Elizabeth. Harding's interest in her is troubling, and I don't know how to protect her without overstepping my bounds."

He paused, emotion welling up within him. "And Charlotte... she is growing so fast, and I worry about her future. She needs guidance and love, and I feel so inadequate at times. You were always the better parent. The one who knew just what to say and do. I miss you more than words can express."

James' voice trembled as he continued, "I never thought I would care for another woman after losing you. But now, with Olivia, I am conflicted. The feelings I have for her are so strong, and yet, I don't know if I have the right to pursue them. I fear I will fail her. Fail them both."

He looked around the garden, where Elizabeth's spirit seemed to linger, and took comfort in the beauty she had created. "Please, give me a sign, Elizabeth. Show me how to navigate this. Help me find the strength and wisdom to do what is right by Olivia and Charlotte. I need your guidance now more than ever."

As he spoke, the wind rustled through the roses, bringing momentary peace. He remained kneeling, eyes closed, hoping for clarity and strength to face the challenges ahead.

Chapter Seventeen

Olivia spent the entire night in the throes of illness, each wave of nausea hitting her harder than the last. It was a relentless cycle, one that left her feeling drained and utterly miserable. The physician had recommended bedrest and herbal teas, and laudanum if she couldn't sleep, and left her in the care of the housekeeper and Jane.

The only respite she found was in the fleeting moments of sleep that came between bouts of sickness. During those brief periods of rest, she clung to the hope that she might wake up feeling better only to be disappointed each time she was jolted awake by another wave of nausea.

Attempting to fathom what could have caused her sudden illness, Olivia thought back to the food she had eaten. Nothing stood out as particularly risky or different from her usual fare. And as far as she knew, no one else in the household was experiencing similar symptoms. It was a puzzle, one that left her feeling even more frustrated and helpless.

On top of the sickness, her body ached in a way she couldn't understand. Every muscle seemed to protest, adding to her discomfort and making it impossible to find a position that offered any relief. Her body was rebelling against her, and she had no idea what she had done to deserve such misery.

By the time morning light began to filter through the curtains,

Olivia was exhausted, both physically and emotionally. The night had been a long, harrowing ordeal, one that she hoped she would never have to endure again. As she finally drifted into a more peaceful sleep, she prayed that the worst was over and that she would wake up feeling like herself once more.

When Olivia awoke next, she found Jane by her bedside, urging her to drink chamomile tea. Olivia took a few sips, hoping the tea would help settle her stomach.

It didn't work. Poor Jane had to grab another basin and shove it under her head for her to expel the little she had consumed, her body wracked with convulsions. It was a disheartening setback, and she crawled back into bed, feeling weaker than ever.

"It's odd that you have no fever." Jane's brow furrowed. "And no one else in the house has fallen ill. Peculiar. But the physician is returning later this morning."

Olivia nodded, too exhausted to respond. The lack of fever was indeed peculiar, adding another layer of mystery to her illness. She lay there, trying to make sense of her symptoms, but her mind was too foggy, too preoccupied with the relentless nausea.

Jane left and Olivia closed her eyes, praying for relief. The sickness had taken a toll on her, both physically and mentally. What on earth was wrong with her? The absence of a fever was a small consolation, but it did little to ease her discomfort or her growing sense of unease.

The doctor was a kind-faced man with a gentle demeanour, and Olivia felt a flicker of hope that he might be able to provide some answers. As he inquired about her symptoms, she responded meekly, her voice barely above a whisper. She detailed the relentless nausea, the vomiting, and the aches that plagued her body.

After a thorough examination, the doctor gave her a reassuring smile. "I'm still confident it will pass in a day or two." He made a few notes. "Just make sure to stay hydrated and get plenty of rest. Most importantly, take the laudanum to sleep. It will help you recover."

Olivia nodded, but how was she supposed to stay hydrated when everything that touched her lips came back up? The idea that this intense sickness would simply pass seemed optimistic, but she clung to the doctor's words, desperate for any promise of relief. She thanked him weakly as he packed up his bag, feeling slightly more hopeful than before.

As the doctor left, Olivia settled back into bed, determined to follow his advice. She sipped water slowly, trying to keep it down, and focused on the thought of feeling better in a day or two. It was a small comfort, but in her current state, it was enough to keep her going.

Two days passed, and Olivia gradually began to feel a little better. The relentless nausea started to subside, and she found she could keep small sips of water down without immediately feeling the urge to vomit. Her body ached less, and she could move around with more ease, no longer feeling like every muscle was rebelling against her.

Each small improvement felt like a victory, a sign that the worst was behind her. She was still far from her usual self, but the progress was encouraging. Olivia took the doctor's advice to heart, resting as much as possible and staying hydrated, hopeful that she would soon be fully recovered.

What mattered most was the fact that she began to feel more like herself. The sickness that had gripped her so fiercely was loosening its hold, and she looked forward to the day when she could resume her duties and spend time with Charlotte without the shadow of illness hanging over her. It was a slow process, but Olivia was patient, grateful for each step toward recovery.

One morning, as Olivia sat in her room still weak but feeling marginally better, a letter arrived from Eleanor. She tore open the envelope, eager for news from home. The letter was filled with well-wishes and updates, and warmth spread through her at her sister's words until she read a sentence that made her heart stop.

Eleanor wrote that she was glad to hear Olivia was recovering, adding, *For a second, I thought you might be with child, since your symptoms sounded like those of a friend who is also with child.*

Olivia's hands trembled as she dropped the letter, her mind racing. The possibility of pregnancy had not even crossed her mind. She tried to remember the last time she had her menses, but the dates were a blur. Panic began to set in as she realised she couldn't recall when it was.

She paced the room, her thoughts a whirlwind of confusion and fear. The implications of a pregnancy were enormous, not just for her, but for James and Charlotte as well. She thought back to the night of the ball, to the moments she and James had shared, and a sinking feeling settled in her stomach.

How could she find out for sure, apart from waiting for her next cycle to put an end to the uncertainty that was gnawing at her.

Olivia forced herself to take a deep breath, trying to calm her racing heart. She needed to think clearly to plan her next steps. But as she stood there, alone in her room, the weight of the situation threatened to overwhelm her.

She tried to reassure herself that there was no need to worry. It was normal for her cycle to be delayed, especially given the illness she had just endured. She convinced herself that the sickness had thrown her body off balance, and that her menses would start soon.

It had to.

As the days passed, Olivia's health continued to improve, but nausea persisted in the mornings, a nagging reminder of her fears. She could only stomach broth, and even that was a struggle at times. It was a concerning development, but she kept her worries to herself, determined not to let them interfere with her duties.

James interrupted their lesson one morning and took Olivia aside, his brow furrowed with concern. "Olivia, you still look quite pale." His gaze lingered on her face. "And are eating very little. Are you sure you're feeling better?"

Olivia forced a smile, trying to appear nonchalant. "Oh, I'm much better, thank you. I suppose my appetite just has not fully returned yet."

He watched her for a moment, clearly unconvinced. "If you're still unwell, you must rest. Charlotte and I can manage without you for a few days."

"No, no, I insist. I'm perfectly capable of continuing with Charlotte's lessons." Olivia winced at the hint of desperation creeping into her voice. She could not afford to take time off, not when she needed the distraction of her work more than ever.

James nodded, though he still looked concerned. "Very well, but please take care of yourself. If you need anything, don't hesitate to ask."

Olivia nodded, relieved that he had not pressed further. She turned her attention back to Charlotte, immersing herself in the lesson, hoping it would be enough to keep her mind off the growing anxiety within her.

Each day was a battle between hope and fear. Olivia clung to the hope that her body was simply recovering from the illness, while the fear that she might be pregnant loomed ever larger in her mind. She could not bring herself to voice her concerns to anyone. Instead, she kept her worries locked away, a silent burden that just kept growing heavier.

At the end of the week, Olivia sat in her room, her mind full of fog. Jane interrupted her wool gathering with a tray of tea and little cinnamon biscuits, soft, fragrant and fresh from the oven.

"Miss, may I be forward with you?" Jane asked, her voice low and hesitant, nothing like normal Jane at all. She wrung her hands nervously, clearly unsure of how to broach the subject on her mind.

"Of course, Jane." Olivia patted Jane's hand. "We've been together long enough for a little forwardness every now and then. Please don't be nervous."

"Are you feeling quite right?" Jane hesitated, blushed to the tips of her ears then took a deep breath. "Your appetite has not recovered, and...and you haven't started your monthlies yet, Miss. It's been near seven weeks now."

Olivia paled. She tried to dismiss the concern with a wave of her hand, but her voice faltered as she spoke. "I'm sure there's a reasonable explanation for it."

But as the reality of the situation settled in, Olivia could no longer hold back the tears. She realised she couldn't lie about it anymore, not to Jane, and not to herself. The possibility of being pregnant was no longer a distant fear, it was a very real possibility that she had to face. She began to cry, the weight of the situation overwhelming her, and Jane rushed to her side, offering comfort and a shoulder to lean on.

Chapter Eighteen

Olivia's health was improving, her colour was returning, and she seemed to have more energy. But she still wasn't eating enough. She would often push her plate away after only a few bites, a look of discomfort on her face. And she still was not herself.

After supper that evening, James turned to Olivia with a polite smile. "Would you care to join me for a walk, Lady Olivia?"

Charlotte frowned. "I want Lady Olivia to read to me. She promised."

James turned to his daughter with a raised eyebrow. "Lady Olivia will still read to you after you get ready for bed."

Charlotte scowled, crossing her arms over her chest and pouting, but she did not argue further. Her nanny soon came to escort her to her room, leaving James and Olivia alone.

There was a slight awkwardness between them, a remnant of their recent interactions, but James pushed it aside. He had to mend the distance he had created between them. Perhaps a walk would be the start of a smoother path ahead.

"Shall we?" James extended his arm to Olivia.

She hesitated for a moment before gently placing her hand on his forearm, a slight tremor in her touch. Was it a testament to the weakness she was still battling, or a reaction to his closeness?

He led her outside, into the cool evening air. The sky was painted with hues of pink and orange as the sun began its descent, casting a soft glow over the manor grounds. Olivia's grip on his arm tightened slightly as they stepped onto the gravel path, and he glanced at her, making sure she was comfortable.

As they walked, James pointed to a vibrant cluster of blooms. "You see those roses over there? They're a new addition. I thought they would add a nice touch of colour to the garden."

Olivia's gaze followed his gesture, and a faint smile appeared on her lips. "They're beautiful."

James nodded, pleased by her response. He guided her attention to another area of the garden. "And over there are the pruned and re-potted lavender bushes. The scent is quite remarkable when they bloom."

"It feels like so long ago that I first came here and fell in love with these gardens." Olivia laughed. "I had almost forgotten how comforting these walks are."

As they continued their walk, Olivia turned to him. "James, have you ever thought of having more children?"

"What? No." His reaction was immediate and sharp. "The duchess and I were satisfied with Charlotte."

Olivia flinched at his response. Guilt shot through his stomach as pain tightened his chest. He softened his tone. "Were satisfied. Before she..." He cleared his throat, unable to finish the sentence.

"Do you ever think about what the future holds for Charlotte?" Olivia asked gently. "She will grow up, marry, perhaps have children of her own. Does that not make you wish for a larger family, for Charlotte as much as for yourself? I wouldn't part with my sisters for the world."

James looked away, the weight of his grief and fear pressing down on him. "I have no intention of marrying again, let alone having another child." His voice tightened with emotion. "I've already married once, and I have no intention of doing it again. I have already lost one wife. I will not lose another."

Olivia sighed and rubbed at her temples as if sensing the depth of his pain but also feeling a twinge of frustration at his closed-mindedness. She drew in a deep breath. "James, I understand your fear, but life goes on. It must. You cannot shut yourself off from the possibility of happiness because of the pain you've endured. Because of the fear of experiencing pain again."

His eyes narrowed, a defensive edge to his voice. "You think it's that simple? That I can just replace Elizabeth and move on as if nothing happened?"

Olivia's patience frayed. "No, I do not think it's simple. But I do think that living in the past does a disservice to the present, and to those who care about you."

James felt a surge of offence. "Charlotte is my responsibility. My duty is to her, to ensure her future is secure."

"And what about me?" Olivia asked, her voice quivering with emotion. "Do I not matter in your world of duties and responsibilities?"

James was taken aback. "Olivia, you are... You are important to me. But this is different."

"Different how?" Her eyes flashed with anger. "Because I am not your daughter? Because I am not your wife? What am I to you, James?"

He struggled to find the words, his emotions in turmoil. "You are... You mean a great deal to me, Olivia. More than I can express. But my primary concern must be Charlotte."

Her face hardened, tears glistening in her eyes. "Thank you, Your Grace. At least now I understand my place in your life."

"You're..." He trailed off, unable to articulate the depth of his feelings. He wanted to tell her how much she meant to him, but he was paralysed by the fear of giving voice to his emotions, of acknowledging how much he had to lose.

"I'm nothing to you." Her breath hitched.

James reached out, but she stepped back, the hurt evident in her posture. "Olivia, please. I did not mean to belittle you. I just... I fear losing anyone else."

"It is not fear that drives you, James," she said, her voice breaking. "It's your inability to see beyond your own pain, to recognise that others might care for you, that they might want to be a part of your life."

Olivia started laughing, but it was a hollow sound, devoid of any real mirth. "I never expected you to love me," she murmured, her voice barely audible. "In fact, I didn't quite know what I expected from you at all. But it was not this."

"Olivia." His voice thickened with emotion. He wanted to make things right, and undo the hurt he had caused, but he didn't know how.

Before his eyes, Olivia changed. She blinked away her tears, and her eyes turned to steel. In that moment, James knew he had lost her. "I think," she said, her voice steady, "I need to visit my family."

"Olivia, please don't leave."

"I'm not. I would never do that to Charlotte. But I think, given these circumstances, it's important for me to clear my head in order to recover fully. Thank you for the walk, Your Grace. However, I'd like to read to Charlotte as promised, and then I will send word to my sister to receive me in three days."

"So soon?" The reality of her departure hit him hard.

"The sooner I get over this, the better."

She wasn't just talking about her illness. She was talking about getting over him, over the hurt and the confusion he had caused. She turned and walked away, leaving James standing alone in the garden, his heart heavy with regret and the realisation of how deeply he had hurt her.

As promised, Olivia left three days later with Jane. The house, once filled with her laughter and lively presence, felt empty without her. Charlotte, who had grown so attached to Olivia, was miserable in her absence. She would often wander to Olivia's room, hoping for a glimpse of her beloved governess, only to be met with the stark reality of her departure.

James, too, felt the weight of Olivia's absence. The manor, his home, felt less like a sanctuary and more like a mausoleum, echoing with the memories of what had been. He found himself wandering through the garden, past the roses Olivia had admired, and felt a pang of longing that surprised him with its intensity.

The days passed slowly, and James began to understand the depth of his feelings for Olivia. It was a discovery that came with a sense of regret and a bitter taste of what could have been. He missed her presence, her laughter, and the way she challenged him. He missed the easy companionship they had shared, and the potential for something more that he had so carelessly dismissed.

Charlotte's sadness was a constant reminder of Olivia's impact on their lives. James did his best to comfort his daughter, but there was a hollowness to his efforts. He couldn't fill the void Olivia had left, and it pained him to see Charlotte so heartbroken.

As the days turned into weeks, James found himself reflecting on his actions and the choices he had made. He realised too late that his attempt to protect himself from the pain of loss had only led to a different kind of heartache. The absence of Olivia had left a void in his life that he was unsure how to fill. It was a lesson learned in the harshest of ways, and one he would not soon forget.

At the dinner table at the end of the second week of Olivia's absence, Charlotte looked across at her father with a sullen expression. "When is she coming home, Father?"

The word "home" struck James with an unexpected force. Yes, Wallingford Manor had become Olivia's home, a place where she had become an integral part of their lives. That awareness brought a pang of regret, a reminder of what he had lost.

"I don't know." James shrugged.

Watching Charlotte's face crumple at his response was a heart-wrenching sight. He hated seeing his daughter in pain, knowing he was powerless to ease her sorrow.

"Has she not mentioned a return date in her letters?" He guessed not, even though Olivia kept up a steady correspondence with Charlotte.

"No, she just sends me lessons." Charlotte slammed her hand onto the table.

"Charlotte that is unnecessary—"

"Did you cause her to leave?"

"I don't know." He had to lie. He couldn't bear to face his daughter's wrath if she learned the truth.

But it was his own heart that broke at the finality of his words. The admission that he didn't know when or if Olivia would return was a bitter pill to swallow. She said she would, and James believed her. Olivia had never lied to him.

But Olivia had never been heartbroken before either.

Not until James broke it for her.

She would come back. He knew she would—for Charlotte.

But when? That uncertainty was something he didn't think he could grapple with.

Chapter Nineteen

Olivia had been at Eleanor and Alexander's home for a fortnight now, her heart heavy with dread. Each day she anxiously awaited her courses, only to be met with disappointment. The nausea was slowly subsiding, a welcome relief after weeks of constant sickness, but exhaustion still weighed heavily on her. Persistent soreness clung to her muscles, a constant reminder of the changes happening within her.

Every morning, it was a struggle to find the energy to start the day. Olivia's thoughts were consumed with worry about the future. If she felt this way now, what would happen when she began to show? The thought of her body changing, her secret becoming visible to all, filled her with a mix of terror and despair.

The consequences of her condition were unthinkable. Her father had already brought shame upon the family with the existence of Caleb, her illegitimate half-brother. The scandal of another illegitimate child would be devastating, not just for her but for the entire family. The social repercussions, the whispers, and the disgrace were unbearable to contemplate.

Olivia had never imagined herself in such a situation, especially under these dire circumstances. She clung to a fragile hope, praying for a miracle that would spare her from the impending scandal and heartache.

She often found herself lost in thought, her hand absently resting on her abdomen, wondering about the life growing inside her. It was a surreal feeling, knowing that she was carrying a child, a part of James. Yes, the future was daunting, but she couldn't help but feel a deep connection to the tiny being she had yet to meet.

Olivia tried to focus on her health and the well-being of her unborn child. Eleanor provided advice and guidance to help Olivia recover. But it seemed no amount of eating nutritious meals and taking gentle walks in the garden would help her.

The day was beautiful, with clear blue skies and a gentle breeze that carried the sweet scent of blooming flowers. Deciding she needed a change of scenery, Olivia stepped outside into the garden, a book in hand. She found a secluded spot under a large oak tree, its branches providing a canopy of shade. Settling down on the soft grass, she opened her book, allowing herself to get lost in the pages.

As she read, the tranquillity of the garden enveloped her, providing a brief respite from the turmoil of her thoughts. The warmth of the sun and the rustling of leaves created a peaceful backdrop, and for a moment, she allowed herself to simply enjoy the beauty of the day.

"Olivia," Eleanor called out softly.

Olivia looked up, surprised to see her sister. She closed her book, a small smile forming on her lips. "Eleanor," she greeted, her voice warm. "It's such a lovely day, isn't it?"

Eleanor smiled back but there was a hint of concern in her eyes.

"It is." Eleanor sat beside Olivia. "But I think we need to talk. I'm worried about you, and I want to understand why you're still here."

Olivia looked up, feigning confusion. "What do you mean?" Olivia tried to mask her emotions. "You know how much I enjoy reading."

Eleanor sighed, her concern palpable. "Olivia, you know full what I meant. You've been here for a fortnight now, and you're not yourself. You're tired, you're distant, and you're avoiding any talk of returning to Charlotte. Your letters were always full of love and concern for that child. What happened?"

Olivia tried to hold back, but the concern in Eleanor's eyes was too much. Her resolve crumbled, and the weight of her secret became too heavy to bear. The lump in her throat grew, and her chest tightened painfully. With tears brimming in her eyes, she finally broke down and confessed everything.

"I'm enceinte, Eleanor," she whispered, the words barely audible. "I'm carrying the duke's child."

The confession hung in the air between them. Olivia had been so afraid to share her secret, but it felt good to finally unburden herself. A mix of relief and dread swirled in her chest, her heart pounding.

Eleanor's initial shock quickly morphed into a fierce protectiveness, her eyes blazing with anger. "Did he take advantage of you?" Her tone was sharp and ready for battle. "Just wait until I tell Alexander. Duke or not, that man will regret ever laying a finger on you."

Olivia's heart raced and she grabbed Eleanor's hand. "It didn't happen like that, Ellie. I wanted it. It wasn't just him."

Eleanor's anger faltered. She leaned forward, her voice low and urgent. "You...you wanted to lie with him?" Her brows knit together as she tried to make sense of Olivia's words.

With a heavy heart, Olivia nodded, the tears she had been holding back spilling over. "I'm in love with him." Words poured out like a dam breaking. Her shoulders shook as sobs racked her body, the reality of her situation crashing down on her. Shame and fear gnawed at her insides, the enormity of her confession leaving her breathless.

Eleanor, still reeling from the revelation, quickly shifted from anger to compassion. She wrapped her arms around Olivia, pulling her into a tight embrace. "Oh, Olivia," she whispered, her voice soft and soothing. "We'll figure this out together. You're not alone. Never, ever alone."

"I will bring so much shame on the family, on myself, on this poor innocent life I carry." Olivia choked out, her voice trembling with despair.

"Shush now. We will work out a way, I promise."

Olivia clung to Eleanor, her mind a whirlwind of emotions. She felt the weight of her fears, the looming shadow of scandal, and yet, in Eleanor's arms, there was a glimmer of hope, a promise of support and love that she desperately needed.

"It hurts, Ellie." Olivia glanced at Eleanor, her eyes glistening with tears. "Is this what you felt with Alexander? This pain? I didn't want to fall in love because I was afraid of being controlled and losing my autonomy. But I never expected so much pain."

Eleanor's eyes softened. "Love can hurt. But with Alexander, it was different. Yes, there was fear, and yes, there was pain, but there was also a deep sense of belonging and understanding. Love isn't just about the joy, it's about weathering the storms together."

The words resonated with Olivia. She had always prided herself on her ability to stand alone. But now, faced with the reality of her feelings for James, she realised that love was a force beyond her control, a force that could bring both immense joy and deep pain.

She wiped away her tears, trying to find strength in her sister's words. "I didn't expect to fall in love, especially not with him."

Eleanor squeezed her hand, offering a silent promise of support. "Love has a way of surprising us," she said, a knowing smile on her lips. "Does he feel the same for you?"

"He does not." Olivia's breath hitched. "At least, he's never said as much. He's still hopelessly devoted to his wife."

"She passed a while ago, didn't she?"

"Almost four years," Olivia muttered, trying not to be jealous of a ghost. "I can't compete with that, Elle. I don't want to. I just... I want him to love me."

"I know." Eleanor pulled Olivia in for another hug. "And that's what you deserve. We'll figure this out. I promise."

Over the next week, Eleanor arranged for a midwife to come to the house discreetly and check on Olivia. She understood the need for secrecy and delicately handled the situation with care. When the day came for the midwife's visit, Olivia was a bundle of nerves. She had so many questions and fears about what lay ahead.

The midwife was kind and gentle, putting Olivia at ease with her calm demeanour. After a thorough examination, she confirmed that it was still early in the pregnancy, but the presence of nausea was a good sign that the baby was continuing to grow healthily. The news brought a sense of relief to Olivia, a small reassurance amid so much uncertainty.

Once the midwife left, Olivia found herself alone with her thoughts. She had never envisioned herself in this situation, had never planned for motherhood at this juncture in her life. And yet, as she sat there, hand resting on her abdomen, she felt a growing sense of attachment to the life forming inside her.

Despite being scared and facing the upheaval this would bring to her life, Olivia realized she wanted this. She wanted to be a mother. The thought was both terrifying and exhilarating, it was a realisation that marked the beginning of a new chapter in her life.

She had to think about the future. The truth of her situation demanded practical solutions. She considered the possibility of having the child adopted, knowing it would be the most discreet way to handle the situation and spare her family from scandal. However, the thought of parting with her baby filled her with a profound sadness she couldn't shake.

Could she find someone willing to marry her in order to provide legitimacy for the child? The idea of a marriage of convenience was not entirely foreign in her social circle, but it was fraught with its own challenges. Could she find someone who would accept her and her unborn child without judgment? And even if she could, would it be a loveless union, devoid of the very affection she craved?

As she pondered these possibilities, a wave of determination washed over her. She would speak with Eleanor, seek her counsel, and explore all options available. She could not navigate this alone. The love and support of her sister would be crucial in making the best decision for her and her child's future.

Facing the future would be daunting, but Olivia knew she had the strength to confront it. With Eleanor and her family by her side and a growing resolve within her, she would find a way to protect and provide for her child, no matter what challenges lay ahead.

Later that night, Olivia sat at her desk, a blank piece of parchment in front of her, and a quill in her hand. Instead of lessons and encouragement to learn, she wanted to write to Charlotte and explain her sudden departure, to reassure her that she would return. But the words wouldn't come. She didn't know how to explain the complexities of her situation to a child, or to convey the turmoil in her heart without causing Charlotte more distress. She was dithering, being a coward. It was an uncomfortable parallel to James's own reticence, a trait she had criticised him for.

Frustrated with herself, Olivia forced the tip of the quill onto the parchment, determined to break through her indecision. She wrote of her fondness for Charlotte, of the joy she found in their lessons and their time together. She avoided the details of her own predicament, focusing instead on the promise of her return. It wasn't the whole truth, but it was the best she could offer without revealing the full extent of her situation.

However, Eleanor returned to the room later that evening, her expression serious as she shut the door behind her. "We've talked about everything except how we will face the future and give this child the best start in life possible." She sat on the edge of the small sofa. "We will need to navigate considerable scandal."

Olivia's heart sank at her sister's words. "Are you asking me to leave?"

"Of course not," Eleanor quickly reassured her. "Our family has weathered scandal before. I've spoken to Alexander, and he suggested that you marry quickly to protect yourself and the child."

"I will not marry because I have to." Olivia's lips pursed.

"It's not just yourself that you need to consider. Your child will be ostracized as well. I'm not saying one way is better than the other, I only wanted to offer you the option. Alexander knows someone who would be willing to help. Apparently, you left quite an impression on him at the ball the duke threw a couple of months ago, to the point where even Alexander has heard him speak about you."

Olivia felt herself pale at the implications. "He knows—"

"No," Eleanor interrupted. "But he doesn't have to. He'll marry you, I'm sure of it."

Olivia was set to refuse outright, but she bit her tongue, realising that Eleanor was right. She needed to think not only of herself but of her child now. "Give me time."

"Of course," Eleanor replied, her eyes full of empathy. "But, Olivia, think quickly. You must wed before you show. There isn't much time left for the gambit to succeed."

Chapter Twenty

With Olivia gone, the days at Wallingford Manor seemed to drag interminably. James found himself going through the motions, his mind constantly drifting to thoughts of her. The manor felt empty without her presence, and he missed the sound of her laughter and the lively conversations they used to share. Charlotte, who had always been a source of joy for him, seemed subdued, her own spirits dampened by Olivia's absence.

Managing his estates had once been a welcome distraction, but now James struggled to focus, his thoughts constantly returning to Olivia. Was she as miserable as he was? Had she found someone new? The thought of her considering a future with another man gnawed at him, fuelling a restlessness he couldn't quell.

One dreary autumn day, Debbit tapped on his study door. "Lord Harding, Your Grace."

Damn the man. He had a knack of calling when James really did not feel like talking to anyone. "Send him in, Debbit."

Harding strutted into his study like a rooster and helped himself to a brandy. "Just came by to thank you, James."

"For what, Harding? I've no idea what you are talking about."

"You must have put in a good word for me. Lady Olivia has invited me to dine with her and the family at Weston's home." The smug grin threatened to stretch his face permanently. "It seems she's finally come around to the idea of my courtship."

James' hands clenched into fists at his sides as he listened. The thought of Olivia entertaining this man, even considering him as a potential suitor, ignited a fierce jealousy within him. How could she think of being with someone else after everything they had shared?

Although, he could not blame her. After how he treated her, he could understand her need to ensure her own protection, especially since James wouldn't.

Unable to contain his emotions, James declared an urgent meeting he needed to attend and all but hustled Harding from his home. He couldn't bear the thought of Olivia with that man, and he was determined to confront her and find out the truth for himself.

And maybe, just maybe, make things right.

"Debbit, organise the carriage. I will be staying at the townhouse for a few days."

The townhouse in Mayfair was kept in a state of readiness for all the occasions he attended parliament. Debbit would send one of the footmen ahead to warn them he was on his way. All he needed to do was to have his valet pack a bag and say farewell to Charlotte. He'd have to concoct a story. If she knew he intended to see Olivia, she would want to tag along.

The carriage ride to Alexander's home was a blur, his thoughts consumed by the need to speak with Olivia. He knew he had no right to demand explanations, no right to insert himself into her life again after everything that had transpired, but to hell with it. He just wanted to see her again.

His heart raced as he arrived at the Weston estate. He was unsure of what he would find or what Olivia would say, but he knew he had to face whatever it was. He couldn't continue living in this state of uncertainty, tormented by the thought of her with someone else.

He was ushered into the drawing room where he found Olivia sitting by the window, her figure bathed in the soft afternoon light. She looked up, surprise etched on her face as she saw him. For a moment, James was struck by her beauty and the way she seemed to belong in that serene setting. But he quickly pushed those thoughts aside, focusing on the reason he was there.

"Lady Olivia, I need to know what's happening. I've heard things, rumours about you entertaining suitors. I need to hear the truth from you."

He waited, his gaze locked on hers, searching for any sign of what she might be feeling. He knew he was treading on dangerous ground and he might not like what he heard. But h needed to know where he stood in her heart. Damn it, first he'd pushed her away, and now all he could think of was how to find a way back to her.

Olivia's furrowed brow deepened. "You came to see me because you heard rumours?" Disbelief coloured her tone. "That's... it?"

It occurred to James how his words must have sounded, how selfish and possessive they seemed. "I meant I wanted to see you—"

Olivia cut him off, standing to face him with a mixture of hurt and indignation in her eyes. "You were fine to let me be until you heard I might be entertaining suitors?" Her voice rose. "You have some nerve."

Frustration surging, James clenched his teeth to try and restrain his emotions.

"I told you how I felt." Olivia's voice trembled with emotion. "I tried to speak to you, but you pushed me away, and now you think you can simply come to my home and demand answers. How dare you."

Her words struck him like a blow, a painful reminder of his own failures, of the distance he had created between them. He stood there, unable to find the words to defend himself, understanding the depth of the hurt he had caused.

"Is it true?" James took a step forward, his eyes searching hers for any hint of deception. "Are you truly trying to find someone else?"

"What would you have me do? I made a reckless mistake, and now..." She let her voice trail off. "I have to think about my future."

"You could come back." His words tumbled out in a rush. "Stay at the manor. I'll protect you."

Olivia's response was immediate and firm. "But not as my husband."

James looked away, the truth of her words stinging. "I didn't think you wanted marriage at all. Isn't that what you told me?"

The room was filled with a tense silence as they both grappled with the reality of their situation, the choices they had made, and the consequences they now faced.

"I appreciate your concern, Your Grace, but I think you should go." Olivia sat as if in dismissal. "And no, I have no intention of wedding your colleague. My brother-in-law thought he was helping, but once I found out, I informed him that I was not interested in trapping anyone in a marriage he did not want."

"Olivia," James murmured, his voice soft with emotion. "Charlotte misses you. She asks for you."

Olivia clenched her teeth, her chin trembling slightly. It was clear she was hurting, the pain of separation from Charlotte adding to her own turmoil. "I doubt you will want me to return."

"Of course, I want you to—"

Olivia cut him off. "I'm with child." She placed her hand on her stomach, a protective gesture that spoke volumes.

James felt as if the ground had shifted beneath his feet. The implications of her words, the reality of their situation, hit him with the force of a tidal wave. The woman he loved—and yes, he admitted it to himself fully, he loved her—the woman he had pushed away, was carrying his child. The enormity of it all left him speechless, struggling to comprehend the depth of the change their lives were about to undergo.

His initial reaction to Olivia's revelation was an overwhelming surge of joy and happiness. The thought of a child, his child with Olivia, filled him with a sense of wonder and excitement he had not expected. For a moment, he allowed himself to indulge in the possibility of a future, a family with the woman he loved.

But as quickly as the joy came, it was replaced by a wave of guilt. He berated himself for losing control that night and not being more cautious. He should have taken better care of the situation and have thought about the consequences of their actions. And now, because of his carelessness, Olivia had been left to endure the repercussions alone.

He had failed Olivia when she needed him most. He had let his own fears and reservations dictate his actions, and in doing so, he had left her to face an uncertain future on her own. That knowledge was a bitter pill to swallow, and it left him grappling with a sense of responsibility he knew he had to face.

"How do I make this better?" James closed the distance between them. "We should marry before—"

"What?" Olivia recoiled as if his words were a physical blow. "No. Absolutely not. We're not going to marry."

James couldn't hide his shock. "You can't be serious."

"I refuse to marry you because you feel obligated. I won't trap you in a marriage you don't want. I will weather the scandal, move to the north in one of Alexander's estates. At least that way, I won't take down my family."

"No." James' voice rose with emotion. "This child is mine as much as it is yours."

"You are under no obligation—"

"I want to be." His gaze locked onto hers. "Do you not understand that? I want to be obligated to you, Olivia. I've wanted you since the moment I saw you."

Olivia's eyes widened in disbelief. "You have made it clear—"

James held up his palms to stop her from speaking further. He had made his position clear to her, and now she deserved a full explanation. He glanced at the carpet, the words he was about to say weighing heavily on his heart.

"When I lost Charlotte's mother, it was devastating." He swallowed a hard lump in his throat. "I vowed I would never endure that again. It is too painful. And I was good at keeping that promise. I kept Charlotte from that burden as well." He paused, gathering his thoughts. "But I've realised that pushing painful feelings away does not get rid of the longing. Charlotte yearns for stories of her mother. In your absence, I've begun to tell her. I thought it would hurt, but it doesn't. It feels good to talk about her."

"I'm glad," Olivia said softly, her voice laced with genuine empathy.

James looked up, meeting her gaze. "What hurts is your absence." The raw truth of his words hung in the air. "More than anything, it's that I've lost you. I thought by pushing you away, I had guarded myself from you, from hurting again, but, in fact, the opposite happened." He took a deep breath, his next words a plea from the depths of his soul.

"Please, Olivia. I must accept your decision, I know. But if you won't agree to marry me, at least come home. For Charlotte's sake. She loves you. Perhaps even more than I do."

James held his breath, waiting, hoping for Olivia to answer. The silence stretched between them, each second feeling like an eternity as he waited for her response.

"I will think about it," she finally said, her voice steady but with an undercurrent of emotion. "Come back tomorrow, and I shall have my answer then."

James wanted to plead his case further, but it wasn't fair to push her. He had to respect her need for time and space to make her decision.

With a heavy heart, he bowed his head and left, the weight of uncertainty pressing down on him as he stepped out into the cool evening air. The walk back to his carriage was a blur, his mind consumed with thoughts of Olivia, of the future, and of the hope that she would choose to come home.

Chapter Twenty-One

As soon as James left, Olivia broke down crying, the weight of her emotions finally catching up to her. Eleanor rushed in at the sound, her eyes wide with concern. "What happened?"

"I love him, Eleanor!" Olivia sobbed, her heart aching with the admission. "I didn't want love to hurt like this." The words tumbled out, a confession of the turmoil she felt inside.

Eleanor's expression softened as she took her sister into her arms. "This stress isn't good for the baby, darling. Try to calm yourself. What happened, Olivia?"

"I told James that I'm pregnant."

Eleanor's eyes widened in shock, but she remained silent, urging Olivia to continue.

"And then he asked me to marry him."

Olivia hiccupped in the comfort of Eleanor's hug.

Seconds passed until Eleanor prodded, "And?"

"But I know he's still in love with his wife, and I'll never live up to that," Olivia whispered.

Eleanor rubbed her back soothingly, trying to offer some comfort. "What did you say? To the proposal?"

Olivia wiped her tears, her voice barely above a whisper. "I told him I need time to think."

"Tell me what to do, Ellie." Olivia's gaze searched her sister's for guidance. "What should I do?"

Eleanor sighed, a look of empathy on her face. "As much as I would love to give you advice, I will not," she said gently. "Other than to follow your heart. Do not betray yourself for what you should do."

"But you said the baby—"

"It's something very important to consider. But that doesn't mean you must completely sacrifice your own needs for love and affection."

Olivia shook her head, a sense of resignation weighing heavily in her voice. "I cannot compete with the ghost of Charlotte's mother. He loved her so much."

"I doubt James would have opened his heart to you if you were a mere replacement, Liv. Take some time and think. We'll be here for you no matter what you decide." Eleanor stood, offering Olivia a reassuring smile. "Take a nap or a walk. Just please do not let your own insecurities drown out the feelings behind the proposal James has offered you."

With those words, Eleanor excused herself and left the room, leaving Olivia alone with her turbulent thoughts.

Seeking solace and perhaps some guidance, Olivia stepped outside for a walk. The cool evening air brushed against her skin, and the gentle rustling of leaves created a soothing backdrop. As she wandered through the gardens, her mind turned to James's late wife, the woman whose presence lingered like a ghost in his life and now, in hers. The weight of the past pressed down on her, almost suffocating in its intensity.

In a moment of desperation, Olivia sat on a stone bench and gazed at the lilac-coloured sky. She found herself speaking silently to the woman she had never met. "What should I do?" Her whisper was carried away by the wind, leaving her feeling even more lost and alone.

She hoped for a sign, some indication from the universe about the path she should take. The idea of marrying James and stepping into the shoes of his beloved wife filled her with a sense of trepidation. How could she ever compare to the memory of a woman he had loved so deeply? The fear of being a mere replacement, a shadow in the light of his past love, gnawed at her. Could she ever truly be enough, could their love ever be free of the chains of the past? The uncertainty of it all weighed heavily on her, a burden she wasn't sure she could bear.

No sign came to guide her, so he she walked on, her thoughts drifting to James, and the look in his eyes when he had confessed his feelings, to the pain in his voice when he spoke of his loss. His heart was not as closed off as she had thought, but reopened, vulnerable and tentative. Could she be the one to help him heal? Could they build a new life together? The thought filled her with an exhilaration she had never dreamed possible.

As the sun dipped below the horizon, casting a warm glow over the gardens, Olivia realized that the answer would not come easily. She had to think practically. The idea of giving the child up for adoption crossed her mind, but the thought was unbearable. This child was a part of her, and the connection she felt was already too strong. Finding someone to marry, someone who would accept her and the baby, seemed a daunting task. But the thought of raising the child alone and facing society's scorn and her family's shame were equally terrifying.

She would need to search deep within herself, to confront her fears and insecurities, and decide if the love she felt for James was strong enough to overcome the obstacles in their path.

Close to the house, Oliva was almost bowled over by her younger sisters.

"Why are you upset?" Mary's brow furrowed in concern.

"I have a lot on my mind." Olivia tried to move around them.

"Like what?" Caroline stood her ground.

Olivia hesitated before answering. "I don't know what I'm meant to do with my life, I suppose."

As she spoke, Olivia thought about her mother, how she was still in pain because of her father's affair. She didn't want that kind of heartache for herself, to be trapped in a loveless marriage or to be forever shadowed by betrayal.

"That's easy." Caroline bounded with youthful confidence. "Just do what you want."

"It's not that simple." Mary's tone was cautious.

"Why not?" Caroline challenged. "When I'm older, I will know exactly what I want, and I won't be afraid to go after it."

Olivia couldn't help but smile at her sister's determination. If only life's decisions were as clear-cut as Caroline believed. But her words echoed in Olivia's mind, a reminder that perhaps there was a simple truth to be found in following her heart.

The rest of the day passed excruciatingly slowly, each hour stretching out like an eternity as Olivia grappled with her decision. She was torn, unsure of what the right answer was, and the weight of her indecision pressed heavily on her heart. She prepared for bed, her mind still racing with thoughts of James, her future, and the child she carried. *Their* child, for James was right. It was his child too. Charlotte's brother or sister.

A single tear escaped and rolled down her cheek. She was tired of pining for what she didn't have. Of being trapped in a cycle of what-ifs and uncertainties. She decided to shift her focus. Instead of dwelling on her fears, she whispered a prayer of gratitude. She was thankful for her family, their unwavering support and love, and for the healthy baby growing inside her.

Her family's love was a constant in her life, bringing a sense of peace, a quiet assurance that she was not alone.

The next morning, Olivia walked in the garden with Caroline and Mary, the fresh air and the sound of their laughing conversation a welcome distraction from the turmoil in her mind. They started chasing one another in a most unladylike fashion, their faces alight with joy. Olivia didn't have the heart to pull them back. Instead, she smiled, genuinely enjoying the moment. She was grateful for the reprieve and the chance to just be present with her sisters, sharing in their joy and laughter.

She heard footsteps and turned to see James approaching.

Her heart skipped a beat, apprehension flooding her. Her breath caught in her throat, and a wave of dizziness washed over her. James was here, earlier than she had expected. She had not yet made her decision. Her pulse quickened, thudding loudly in her ears, and her palms grew clammy with sweat.

"Lady Olivia." James gave a small bow, his smooth baritone breaking through the whirlwind that occupied her head. He cleared his throat, his gaze filled with uncertainty.

The world around them faded into the background, the laughter of her sisters now a distant murmur. Olivia's thoughts raced, colliding with one another in a frantic scramble. This was a turning point. The words spoken in the next few minutes would change the course of her life, of both their lives.

She swallowed hard, trying to steady herself, but her voice trembled when she finally spoke. "James, I... I wasn't expecting you so soon."

Caroline approached James. "Who are you?"

"Let's go." Mary grabbed Caroline's hand and pulled her away, giving Olivia and James a moment of privacy.

Olivia watched her sisters retreat before turning back to James.

"I know," he said gently, his gaze probing hers as if seeking some indication of her thoughts. "But I couldn't wait any longer. I needed to speak with you."

The vulnerability in his voice mirrored her own turmoil, and for a moment, she felt the weight of their shared uncertainty. Could she take this step, embrace this new future with him, despite the ghosts of the past and the fears that haunted her?

"I..." She hesitated, feeling the pressure of the moment bearing down on her. Her hand instinctively moved to her abdomen, a protective gesture over the life growing within her. "James, I'm so afraid."

His expression softened, and he took a tentative step closer. "Olivia, whatever you decide, we will face it together. I promise you that."

The sincerity in his words pierced through her panic, offering a glimmer of hope. She took a deep breath, trying to calm the storm inside her. This was it—the moment of truth. She had to confront her fears and decide if the love she felt for James was strong enough to overcome the obstacles in their path.

"Let's sit," she managed to say, gesturing to a nearby bench. As they moved to sit down, her mind continued to swirl with doubts and possibilities.

"Olivia" James twisted so their knees touched. "I've used my wife's death as a crutch for too long, a way to keep myself free from pain. But in doing so, I isolated myself from the possibility of happiness. You changed that. You ruined it, in the best possible way. I was drawn to you whether I wanted to be or not. And now, I can't imagine my life without you."

He paused, his eyes searching hers. "I'm overjoyed at the thought of being a father again. Forgive my fear, my love. I lost my first wife during childbirth and Charlotte's baby brother lived for just a few days, and I kept them apart. But the thought of being parted from you is unbearable.

He got down onto one knee. "Olivia, will you marry me? Will you give me the chance to spend the rest of my life with you, to be a family with our child and Charlotte?" His words were a heartfelt plea, a confession of his love and his fears, and tears welled in her eyes as she listened.

A weight lifted off her shoulders. The uncertainty and fear that had been clouding her heart gave way to a sense of hope and happiness.

"Yes," Olivia whispered, her voice filled with emotion. "Yes, James. Yes."

James stood, a look of relief and joy spreading across his face. He pulled her in for a surprisingly passionate kiss, his lips making all the promises he hadn't spoken, and pledging a future filled with love. Olivia melted into the embrace, her heart soaring with the knowledge that she had made the right choice, that she and James would face whatever lay ahead together, as a family.

"For the love of God, is it supposed to hurt like this?" Olivia clutched at Eleanor's outstretched hand.

The room was filled with tense anticipation, the air thick with the sounds of her laboured breathing. Eleanor was by her side, offering words of encouragement and comfort. The midwives bustled about, readying themselves, their experienced gazes watching Olivia closely.

"Curse this pain,' she ground out. The contractions came in waves, each one more intense than the last, a relentless tide that left her breathless. The pain was all-encompassing, a primal force that demanded her full attention. She clung to Eleanor's hand, drawing comfort from her sister's unwavering presence as each wave crashed over her.

The midwives were a constant source of guidance, their voices calm and steady amidst the storm of pain. "Breathe, Olivia," they would remind her as a contraction began to build. "Focus on your breathing."

And she would try, drawing in deep, ragged breaths, trying to ride the wave rather than be consumed by it.

Screaming helped.

As the labour progressed, the moments between contractions grew shorter, the intensity of the pain deepening. "You're doing beautifully, Olivia," the midwife encouraged. "Just a bit longer now."

Their words were a lifeline, something to hold onto as her body was wracked with pain.

Then came the time to push, a new kind of challenge. "Push, Olivia, push," they urged, their voices firm and encouraging. She gathered all her remaining strength, pushing with all her might, her body stretched to its limits. The pain was almost unbearable, a searing fire that seemed to fill her entire being.

Nothing happened, and Olivia felt a momentary sense of despair, her body trembling with exertion. "I want James. This is all his fault."

"It's okay," Eleanor's tone was a soothing balm. "You can do this."

Olivia looked down at the ring on her finger, a tangible reminder of James, of her husband who was waiting just outside. She couldn't let her family down. Not him. Not Charlotte. And certainly not this baby. The thought of them, of the love they shared, bolstered her spirits and gave her the strength she needed to continue.

"Ready to push again?" The midwife gently wiped Olivia's forehead. "This is quite a large baby, I'm afraid.

"Damn it!" Olivia screamed again. Then, miraculously, the pain subsided, replaced by the sound of a newborn's cry.

The midwives quickly cleaned and wrapped the baby, then placed the little one in Olivia's arms. The moment she looked into her child's eyes, all the pain and fear melted away, replaced by a love so profound it took her breath away.

Eleanor wiped away tears of joy, her smile beaming as she looked at her sister and the new life she had brought into the world. "You did it, Olivia," she whispered, her voice full of awe.

"My baby," Olivia murmured.

"A girl," the second midwife said. "Ten fingers, ten toes. She's beautiful."

"I'll get James." Eleanor kissed first her sister and then her brand new niece and slipped out of the room to fetch James.

Anticipation surged at the thought of James seeing their baby for the first time. She imagined the look on his face, the joy and love that would surely shine in his eyes. It was a moment she had dreamed of that signified the beginning of their journey as a family.

At that moment, James walked in, a wide-eyed Charlotte at his heels.

"Meet your daughter," Olivia said, her voice filled with pride. "Would you like to hold her?"

James hesitated, his concern for Olivia evident. "Are you...are you safe? Are you all right?"

The second midwife gave him a reassuring smile. "She was made for having babies."

With a tentative smile, James reached out to take his daughter in his arms, cradling her with a tenderness that moved Olivia to tears. With his free hand, he took Olivia's, their fingers intertwining. "I love you," he told her, his voice filled with emotion.

"I love you too," she whispered back, her heart swelling with love for her husband and their newborn daughter.

She held out her arms to Charlotte and pulled her into a tight hug.

In that moment, surrounded by her family, Olivia felt a sense of completeness, a deep joy that she knew would stay with her forever.